### Praise for *Hom*

T0268831

"Shot through with dark humor, [...] signature freshness that makes life [...]

"With dark humor and lyrical expansiveness, Barrett's second collection of stories captures the weirdness and beauty of seemingly ordinary lives."
—*New Yorker*, Best Books of 2022 So Far

"Colin Barrett . . . writes what he knows, but he also writes to discover what he doesn't know, a simple but crucial distinction you can sense instinctively, no matter how many of his compatriots you've already read." —*Los Angeles Times*

"Many a writer claims mastery of technique, but few deliver at the level of Colin Barrett, whose roving perspectives, lopped-off endings and Kevin Barry-esque dialogue dazzle in his second collection." —*Minneapolis Star Tribune*

"I'm not ashamed to admit that I'd read Barrett's grocery lists should he choose to publish them." —*Millions*

"Beguiling . . . there isn't a dull page in the book."
—*Highbrow Magazine*

"Superb . . . Barrett is already one of the leading writers of the Irish short story, which is to braggingly say, one of the leading writers of the short story anywhere. He means every word and regrets every word. He just kills it." —*Guardian* (UK)

"A beautiful and moving collection, from one of the best story writers in the English language today."
—*Financial Times* (UK)

"*Homesickness* is another finely crafted collection . . . Crisply told, fond of an eye-catching flourish . . . the stories draw energy from the rhythms of west of Ireland small talk, added to Barrett's eye for striking detail . . . The scenarios are richly layered, with punchy payoffs." —*Observer* (UK)

"Barrett's stories are, without exception, beautifully written, full of arresting imagery." —*Booklist* (starred review)

"Bittersweet and chiseled ... From gritty realism to oddball noir, this assured collection demonstrates the talent of a distinctive writer."                                    —*Publishers Weekly*

"Richly descriptive ... Sharply observant."    —*Kirkus Reviews*

"If there is any concern about the health of the short story in the next generation of Irish writers, Colin Barrett's *Homesickness: Stories*, his second collection, should help put that to rest."
                                                    —*Shelf Awareness*

"In this strong second collection—not a repeat act—readers become involved in the simple but crucial issue of how they will manage."                                    —*Library Journal*

"This is a mesmerizingly powerful book, full of the strangeness and beauty of life. I've learned so much from Colin Barrett's work as a reader and writer, and I think these stories are his best yet."    —Sally Rooney, author of *Normal People*

"A masterwork—by turns hilarious and heart-breaking, these stories shimmer. No story writer at work today thrills me more than Colin Barrett, whose characters feel immediately so familiar and true in their capacity to maim and love. What fierce, tender stories. Totally unforgettable."
                                    —Brandon Taylor, author of *Real Life*

"Something struck me as I read these beautifully crafted, desperately sad, but often very funny stories: there is now a branch of English called the Colin Barrett."
                                    —Roddy Doyle, author of *The Commitments*

"The stories in *Homesickness* are crafted with skill and flair. Colin Barrett anchors the work with emotional accuracy and careful delineation of character, and then, using metaphors and beautifully made sentences, he lets his narrative soar."
                                    —Colm Tóibín, author of *Brooklyn*

"These are addictive, stylish and violently funny stories, with riches on every page—an outstanding collection."
                                    —Kevin Barry, author of *Night Boat to Tangier*

"Edgy, sharp and utterly original, *Homesickness* is an utterly compelling collection and Barrett is meticulous."
                                    —Elaine Feeney, author of *As You Were*

# HOME
# SICK
# NESS

Also by Colin Barrett

*Young Skins*

# HOME SICK NESS

*Stories*

## COLIN BARRETT

Grove Press
*New York*

'A Shooting in Rathreedane', 'The Ways', 'Whoever is There, Come on
Through' and 'Anhedonia, Here I Come' first appeared in the *New Yorker*;
'The Alps' first appeared in *Harper's*. An earlier version of 'The Silver
Coast' was commissioned by RTÉ Radio 1 for SPOKEN STORIES 1:
Independence and first broadcast in 2021

First published in Great Britain in 2022 by Jonathan Cape,
an imprint of Penguin Random House UK.

*Printed in Canada*

First Grove Atlantic hardcover edition: May 2022
First Grove Atlantic paperback edition: May 2023

Typeset by Jouve (UK), Milton Keynes

Library of Congress Cataloging-in-Publication data is available for this title.

ISBN 978-0-8021-6174-1
eISBN 978-0-8021-5965-6

Grove Press
an imprint of Grove Atlantic
154 West 14th Street
New York, NY 10011

Distributed by Publishers Group West

groveatlantic.com

23  24  25  26  27      10  9  8  7  6  5  4  3  2  1

For
Lucy, Ellie & Daniel

# CONTENTS

# A SHOOTING IN RATHREEDANE

S ERGEANT JACKIE Noonan was squaring away paper-work when the call came in, just her and the gosling, Pronsius Swift, in Ballina Garda Station. The third officer on duty, Sergeant Dennis Crean, had run out to oversee the extraction of a Renault Megane some young lad – sober, apparently, just a nervous non-local negotiating the cat's cradle of back roads around Currabbaggan – had nosed into a ditch a half mile out from the national school. The car was a write-off but the lad had got away without a scratch, according to Crean, and he was a lucky lad because Noonan knew the roads out that way and they were wicked; high ditched, hilly and altogether too narrow, scantily signposted and laced with half-hidden, acutely right-angled turns it took only a second's inattention to be ambushed by.

Noonan was at her desk drinking coffee black as a vinyl record from a battered silver cafetière and transferring a weekend's worth of write-ups from her notebook into the central computer system. The weekend had been unre-markable but busy: there had been a dozen or so minor traffic infractions, a fist-fight between stocious teenage cousins outside a main-street chipper late last night and a call-out this morning prompted by what turned out to be a man's empty duffel coat snagged in the weir gates of the Moy river, which was enthusiastically mistaken for a body by a band of visiting American summer students and their professor taking an early constitutional along the quays.

The notes, executed in Noonan's irredeemable *ciotóg* scrawl, were the usual hassle to decipher, their transcription to the computer an activity of an order of tedium Noonan nonetheless found strangely assuaging. So absorbed was she in this task that she started in surprise when the phone on the main desk first rang out.

'Pronsius,' she commanded, without looking away from the screen. The phone continued ringing.

'Pronsius!'

Noonan glanced up. Pronsius wasn't at his desk. He wasn't in the room.

Noonan made her way over to the main desk. She snatched the handset from its cradle.

'Ballina Garda Station, Sergeant Noonan speaking.'

'There's been a shooting,' a voice, a man's, declared.

'A shooting?' Noonan repeated just as Pronsius appeared with a mug in his hand. Pronsius Swift was twenty-four, out of Templemore less than three years, and an aura of adolescent gawkiness clung to him yet; he was tall but disposed to stooping, with an emphatic aquiline bump in his conk, jumpy eyes, and a guileless shine coming off his forehead. Even the chevrons of premature grey in his crew cut served only to emphasise his prevailing boyishness. When he heard Noonan say 'a shooting', he froze in place and stared at her with his mouth open.

'When you say "a shooting" – a shooting as in someone's been shot with a gun?' Noonan asked the man.

'What other kind of shooting is there?' the man said.

'Hang on, now,' Noonan said. Keeping the cordless handset to her ear, she returned to her own desk, sat back down, and retrieved her pen and notebook.

'How many people have been shot?' she asked.

'Just the one.'

'The person shot. A man or a woman?'

'A man.'

'Is he dead?'

The man on the end of the line sighed.

'He is not. He's out there now in the back field. He's in a bit of a bad way.'

'How badly injured is he, in your estimation?' Noonan said, raising a finger to fix Pronsius's attention then pointing at the phone on his desk, meaning *call the emergency at Castlebar General*.

'He took a serious enough hit. But what it was, was a warning shot. I want it on record I was in fear of my life and my son's life. I was not aiming at him at all. He broke on to my property. I was in fear of my life and was only trying to warn him off.'

The man was outside, on a mobile, his voice dipping in and out amid the ambient scratch and crumple of the elements.

'I need your name,' Noonan said, and when the man did not immediately answer she added, 'It's important you answer my questions now, please.'

'Bertie. Bertie Creedon,' the man said.

'Where's your property located, Mr Creedon?'

'Rathreedane. I'm on the far side of Rathreedane.'

'You're going to have to narrow that down for me.'

'Take the Bonniconlon road as far as Mills Turn. Do you know Mills Turn?'

'I do,' Noonan said, dashing down *Mlls Trn* in her notebook. 'Where am I heading from there?'

'Take the third road on the left after Mills Turn. Keep along *that* road a mile and a half until you come to a farm with a yellow bungalow and a '92 Fiat motorhome up on bricks out the front.'

'Yellow bungalow, '92 Fiat motorhome, up on bricks,' Noonan recited as she wrote. 'OK – I have you, your young fella, and the fella's been shot – is there anyone else to account for on the property?'

'That's it.'

'And the injury. How many times was the fella shot?'

'Just the once. By accident. Like I said.'

'Where on his body did he take the hit, can you tell?'

'In his – in his middle. His midriff.'

'What kind a gun was he shot with?'

'A shotgun.'

'Double-barrel?'

'Double-barrel.'

'And that's your gun, is it?'

The growl of a throat-clear, almost gratified-sounding, came down the line. 'It's legally registered and I'm lucky I have it.'

'As far as you can determine, is the man bleeding badly? I don't want you to go prodding at him but it's important to stop the bleeding if you can.'

'The son's after going inside and emptying the press of

every last towel. We have the wounds stanched as best we can.'

'That's good, Mr Creedon. Keep the pressure on the bleeding. We are coming right out. The ambulance is on the way too. What I would ask is that you render your gun safe if you haven't already done so—'

'What happened to this fella is on him,' Creedon interjected with renewed conviction. 'He was on my property, he was in the act of committing a crime and I was in fear for my life and my son's life. I want that clear.'

'O.K. We will be there in fifteen minutes, Mr Creedon. Just heed what I said about the gun. Let's just take the gun out of the equation altogether—' Noonan said, but the quenched noise of the disconnected line was already in her ear.

Noonan dropped the handset on her desk.

'Did you catch all that?' she asked Swift.

'Ambulance is dispatched,' Swift said.

'Let's beat them to the draw,' Noonan said.

Noonan and Swift were on the road when they got Crean on the squad-car radio.

'Shots fired, man down, firearm still in play,' Crean summarised after Noonan had given him a rundown of the situation.

'That's the size of it,' Noonan said.

'I'm wondering if we shouldn't just put a shout in now to the Special Response Unit,' Crean suggested.

'Fella's done the shooting rang us of his own volition. I asked him questions, he answered them. He's not lost his reason.'

'You can't rely on reason with a firearm in play.'

'Just let us put our feet on the ground out there, get the lay of the land. No cause to escalate yet.'

'I'm the other side of Ballina and I'll be out to you as soon as I can. But, Noonan, ye get out there and there's a hint of *anything* off I need ye to withdraw and hold tight.'

'I hear you.'

'Good luck,' Crean said and signed off.

They were a couple of miles out from Mills Turn when they ranged into the wake of a tractor towing a trailer full of sheep. Noonan got right up the trailer's arse, siren *wapwapping*, but the stretch of road they were on was not wide enough for the tractor to let them pass.

'Come on to fuck,' Noonan said as the trailer weaved from side to side ahead of them. Sheep were packed thick into the trailer's confines, stamps of red dye smudged on their coats like bloody handprints, their snouts nudging in anxious query between the gaps in the bars. Once the road opened out, Noonan gunned the engine and streaked by the tractor.

As instructed, they took the third left after Mills Turn and found themselves on the Rathreedane road. Rathreedane was nothing but flat acres of farmland, well-spaced houses set off the road at the ends of long lanes, and cows sitting like shelves of rock in the middle of the fields, absorbing the last of the day's declining rays. Where the ditches dropped low those same rays, crazed with motes and still piercingly bright, blazed across Noonan's sightline. She flipped down the visor. She considered the gosling. Swift had gone quieter than usual, his gaze trained out the window and one knee frantically joggling.

'That is some incarnation of sun,' Noonan said, talking

just to talk, to draw Swift out of his introversion and back into the here and now. 'Haven't seen a sun like that since Guadalajara. You know where Guadalajara is, Pronsius?'

'Is it the far side of Belmullet?'

Noonan smiled.

'Technically it is. Visited there a few years back. Unreal how beautiful it was. The light just lands different.'

'The world is different everywhere, I suppose.'

'We went there for an anniversary. It was Trevor's idea. Trevor's the traveller,' Noonan continued. Trevor was her husband. 'Enjoying the place you get to is one thing. But Trevor has this thing for the travel itself; the luggage and the security lines, the time zones, the little trays of food with the foil lids you peel back they give you onboard, and these days having to drag a pair of mewling teenage boys everywhere with us. Trevor gets giddy at all of it, somehow. Me, I could live a long happy life never going through a metal detector again. You ever been anywhere exotic, Pronsius?'

'I been the far side of Belmullet.'

'Good man.'

'Ah,' Swift sighed, 'I've no interest, really. Wherever I am, that's where I like.'

'A man after my own heart.'


Presently they found the residence, a low bungalow off a gravel lane, the red galvanised roofs of farm buildings visible at the rear of the property. An enormous, rickety white motorhome was stranded in the grass out front.

'Now we'll see what's what,' Noonan said.

She cut the siren and turned through the concrete posts

of the gateless gate. The squad car bounced and lurched as it passed over the rattling bars of a cattle grid. Next to the motorhome there were pieces of outdoor furniture and what looked like a little fire pit dug out of the ground, empty wine bottles planted in the moat of ash ringing the pit. Scattered elsewhere in the grass were bags of feed, a stripped-down, rusted-out engine block, scraps of tarp, scraps of lumber, metal piping, plastic piping, bits and bits and bits.

'Look at all this shit,' Noonan said.

'Steady on,' Swift said with a nod.

A man had come around the side of the house. He was holding something to his head and his other arm was raised, palm forward.

Noonan killed the engine and got out of the squad car, keeping her body behind the door. Swift followed her lead on the other side.

'This the Creedon residence?' Noonan asked.

'It is, surely,' the man said.

He was pressing a stained tea towel of blue and white check to his temple. The stains looked like blood.

'I'm Sergeant Noonan out of Ballina Garda Station. This is Garda Swift. You Bertie Creedon?'

'Christ, no.'

'You'd be the son, then?'

'That's more like it.'

'What's your name?'

'I've no say in it but every cunt that knows me does call me Bubbles.'

Bubbles looked to be in his early thirties. He was stocky, his head shaved close. He was in a faded grey T-shirt with

QUEENS OF THE STONE AGE, ERA VULGARIS printed on it in a disintegrating white script. There were dark wet daubs of blood flecking his forearms like tracks left by a bird.

'We hear there's been a spot of bother,' Noonan said.

'There has.'

'That knock to the head part of the bother?'

'A little bit, all right,' Bubbles said and lifted the towel away from his temple to let them see. There was an open gash above his eyebrow.

Noonan whistled.

'I wager that needs stitching. I understand there's another man in a bad way here too, is that right?'

'There is, yeah.'

'That his blood on you?'

'Some of it, yeah.'

'Can you take us to him?'

'I can.'

'Get the emergency kit,' Noonan said to Swift. Swift popped the boot, took out a bulky, multi-pocketed bag and handed it over to Noonan.

'Lead the way,' she said, sliding the kit's strap over her shoulder.

Bubbles cleared his throat.

'This situation here. You have to understand, my father was in fear for our lives.'

'We'll be sure to take that into account.'

Bubbles led Noonan and Swift down a short dirt track into the yard at the back of the property. The yard was covered in matted, trampled-down straw. Noonan watched

Bubbles step indifferently into a cowpat the size of a dinner plate, his boot heel leaving an oozing bite-mark in the pat's crust. The air was thick with the heavy, grainy-sweet redolence of fodder and shit. Through a window cut out of the galvanised facade of a shed cows blinked their stark, red-rimmed eyes as if roused from sleep.

'That's where we caught him, brazen as you like,' Bubbles said, gesturing at the large, cylindrical oil tank mounted on a bed of brick next to the cowshed.

'He was thieving oil?' Noonan asked.

'Such a stupid thing to be at,' Bubbles said. 'There's nothing left from the winter gone and it won't be filled again for months. Who's going to have a full tank of oil in the middle of summer?'

They passed a final row of sheds and came out into an open field. Fifty feet ahead of them a short man was standing over a second man lying on his back on the ground. On the horizon Noonan could make out the low, blunted serrations of the Ox Mountains.

'Bertie Creedon?' Noonan called out to the standing man.

'Aye,' Creedon said, not taking his eyes off the man on the ground, his shotgun tucked at an idle diagonal under his arm.

Noonan kept walking toward Creedon at an even clip, not hurrying, taking care not to break stride. When she was a handful of paces from him he finally looked at her. Creedon had watery blue eyes, cheeks latticed with broken blood vessels, a head of windblown, thinning yellow hair, and a set of small, corroded teeth. He did not react as Noonan gripped the barrel of the shotgun, brought her second hand to the butt and transferred the weapon into her embrace as firmly and gently as if she were taking possession of a newborn. She checked the safety, broke the gun, slipped the ammunition from the chamber and pocketed the cartridges.

'All right,' Noonan said.

She handed the gun off to Swift, took a second look at Creedon to make sure he wasn't considering anything, then addressed her attention to the man lying in the grass. The man was young, lanky enough by the sprawl of him, his dark hair sticking to his pale forehead in strings, and for a moment Noonan did not recognise him, his features crushed into anonymity with distress. It was only when his eyes, screwed shut, burst fearfully open – they were blue, but a deeper, more charged blue than the farmer's, phosphorescent almost – that his face turned into one Noonan knew.

'God above in Heaven is that you, Dylan Judge?'

Dylan Judge groaned in assent.

Dylan Judge was from Ballina town. He was what you would call 'known to the police'. In his early twenties, he had already run up a decent tally of minor convictions. Breaking and entering, drunk and disorderly, possession; Judge was one of those prolific, inveterately small-time crooks who possessed real criminal instincts but no real criminal talent. He was opportunistic, impulsive and undisciplined, requiring little in the way of convincing – and not even much in the way of incentive – to be roped into an underhanded scheme, so long as the scheme did not require much effort or forethought. Noonan kneeled down in the grass next to Judge and slid the emergency kitbag from her shoulder. She tore open a pack of nitrile gloves, worked the gloves over her hands.

'Do you remember me at all, Dylan?'

Judge looked blankly up at her.

'It's Noonan, Sergeant Jackie Noonan out of Ballina.
And that there is Garda Pronsius Swift.'

'Pronsiusssss,' Judge repeated with a sneer.

'It's a name that draws attention to itself, all right,'
Noonan said as she began scanning Judge's wounds. There
was a mess of hand towels plastered over his groin and
tucked in under his backside. The towels, along with his
jeans, were plum dark with blood. From the amount of
blood, Noonan could tell he was in a very bad way. She
unpacked the gauze, the trauma shears.

'You remember the last time we met?' Noonan asked.
'We were chasing a consignment of cigarettes and wound
up at your house.'

'Ye stormed into the gaff at all hours,' Judge said with
genuine recollection.

'We thought we had you, Dylan.'

'And ye were out of luck.'

'That time, we were.'

It must have been a little over a year ago. They'd
received a tip considered credible that Judge was sitting
on a significant quantity of cigarettes smuggled down
from the North, so they got a warrant and raided his place,
in the Glen Gardens estate. Technically not even his
place, because there was only the girlfriend's name on the
lease, if Noonan remembered correctly. They raided
the house at dawn and made Judge, his girlfriend and their
little daughter stand outside in their pyjamas in the chill
grey light while the Guards turned the place upside down.
Noonan remembered the girlfriend; five foot nothing,

stick thin and incensed, unceasingly effing and blinding while a saucer-eyed and gravely silent little girl, no more than three or four years old, sat up in her arms watching the Guards troop in and out of the house. Not a peep out of this fella that Noonan could remember, Judge just skulking meekly behind his raging *beoir*, eyes on the ground. And though his entire demeanour had read guilty as sin, the raid somehow turned out to be a waste of time. All they found was a half dozen cartons of cigarettes under a tarp in the back of the property's suspiciously empty shed, nowhere near enough to hang an intent-to-sell charge on.

'Are you still with that young one, Dylan? That one with the mouth on her?' Noonan asked. She wanted to keep him awake and talking.

'Amy, yeah. Same bird.'

'Such language out of her, this slip of a thing stood there in her fluffy slippers calling us every name under the sun, and the little beaut good as gold up in her arms. What age is your girl?'

'That's Amy's kid.'

Gingerly, Noonan removed the towels covering Judge's groin. Judge gasped.

'That's OK, that's OK,' Noonan said. 'It doesn't matter a whit whether she's yours or not, so long as you treat her well.'

'I treat her like a queen,' he slurred.

'I bet you do. Bear with me now, Dylan,' Noonan said. She slipped off Judge's runner, lifted the cuff of his trouser leg and with the trauma shears drew a clean slit from his ankle up to his hip and peeled back the panel of the jeans. She could make out several raw black punctures where the buckshot had gone into his thigh. His skin was stained with drying blood and there was fresh blood oozing steadily from the wounds. Noonan continued cutting, tearing delicately away his T-shirt. His abdomen was completely sodden in blood and there were big ugly perforations in the flesh of his stomach, as if he'd been gored. A malign smell began to gather under Noonan's nose. It took her a second to recognise it as the smell of human shit.

'How's it look?' Judge croaked.

'Like you got shot.'

'Ah fuck, am I gonta die?'

'I reckon if you were going to bleed to death, you would have done so by now,' Noonan hedged.

There was little she could do but keep Judge calm and conscious. Steadying her touch as best she could, she began tearing gauze into strips and placing the strips over the worst-looking wounds, watching as each swatch of material was immediately soaked through with a fresh bloom of red. She picked back up one of the towels and pressed it against his abdomen. In close, she heard a small, insistent noise, and there, down in the grass under Judge's head, a racing, paper-thin beat was escaping from an earbud.

'What's the little girl's name?' Noonan asked but Judge did not answer. His eyelids were heavy and fluttering, like those of a child fighting sleep. His lips were colourless, stuck to his teeth.

'Come on now, Dylan,' Noonan asserted, tapping his cheek with her fingers. 'Ambulance'll be here any second. Come on. They're going to pump you full of the good stuff. Pharmaceutical-grade narcotics and no fucking about.'

Noonan thought she saw a smile, a faint flicker on Judge's lips. A few feet away in the grass were tossed a metal bar and a plastic jerrican, a length of hosepipe sticking out of it. Noonan wondered where it was Judge might have been heading, and then she saw it, at the far edge of the field, the squat, muddy white body of a quad bike parked in the declivity of what must have been a boreen.

'See that?' she said to Swift. 'The getaway vehicle.'

She thought about what Bubbles had said in the yard: that summer was the stupidest possible time to try and rob oil out of an oil tank. Noonan had grown up in the countryside. There had been a tank out the back of the house that was filled every autumn, just before the cold weather set in. Although there was always a sitting-room fire going, use of the radiators was strictly rationed. The goal was to try and have the single tank of oil last the whole winter. And so Jackie Noonan's house had been a cold house. Noonan remembered her mother roaring at her and her siblings to put on a jumper whenever one of them dared voice a complaint about the cold. She remembered the single-glaze window above her headboard in the bedroom she shared with her sisters Maureen and Patricia, the brown-putty smell of the fly-specked sill and the clear ache in the tips of her fingers when she touched her hand to the thin glass on winter mornings.

She was holding Judge's arm, two fingers pressed to his wrist. His arm was an alienly cold weight. He was still breathing but she wanted to feel the tick of his pulse under the skin to assure herself it was there. With her other hand, she was keeping a towel pressed against the worst of the bleeding. Beneath his head she could still hear the tiny, tinny *ttt ttt ttt* of his headphones. The miasmic smell of human shit seemed to be getting stronger. She felt as if it were working itself into her pores, coating the back of her throat. Noonan believed Dylan Judge was going to die if the ambulance did not arrive very soon, and probably anyway.

'Here come the cavalry,' Swift said.

Noonan looked up and saw three figures jogging across the field. Sergeant Dennis Crean led the way followed by two paramedics toting a scoop stretcher. Just as he was about to reach them, Crean stumbled and his jog turned into a sudden hobble.

'Shite!' he exclaimed.

'You OK?' Noonan asked.

'I'm after going over my ankle.'

The paramedics dropped down into the grass next to Noonan and Judge.

'We have it now,' one of them said.

Noonan got to her feet and stepped back. She brushed her brow with her gloved hand and felt the cold slickness of blood on her forehead.

'That's Dylan Judge,' she said to Crean, who was grimacing and testing the weight on his foot.

'Are you kidding me,' Crean said, squinting coolly at Judge's white, unconscious face.

Crean had played rugby for Connacht when he was younger. The rim of his left ear was baroquely gnarled, his nose coarsely flattened from repeated breaks. These historical injuries, combined with Crean's big belly and bull neck, suggested vigour and capability. Noonan could hear air being expelled in a slow, thoughtful jet through the crushed passage of his nose, a noise she had always found reassuring.

'Judge was in the middle of robbing the oil tank in the yard when these two interrupted him,' she said.

Crean lifted his foot, rotated it carefully in the air, and put it down.

'Who shot him?'

'Bertie here, the senior of the two, is claiming he did,' Noonan said when neither man spoke.

'I did not mean to,' Creedon said.

Crean chuckled to himself.

The paramedics were preparing to move Judge. They had strapped him to the stretcher and placed an oxygen mask over his face. Crean touched Noonan on the elbow to indicate that she should stay put. He joined the paramedics, exchanging a couple of hushed sentences with one of them before they lifted the stretcher and began making their way toward the yard.

'Is he still alive?' Noonan asked when Crean came back over to her.

Crean's grunt was equivocal.

'I reckon he was just about to go as you got here,' Noonan said.

'That's not your call to make,' Crean said. 'That boy isn't dead until they say he's dead.'

Crean addressed the Creedon men.

'So walk us through what happened here,' he said.

'We'd been away at the mart in Balla,' Creedon said,

'only we came back earlier than usual this afternoon because the young fella was supposed to have football training tonight. We got in and Bubbles went out to the yard to check on the animals.'

'That's when I saw him, brazen as you like, straddling that tank like he was up on a horse,' Bubbles said. 'He'd his back to me. Before I could stop myself I called out *hey!* But he didn't pay me a blind bit of heed.'

Bubbles pointed a finger at the side of his head.

'The fella had headphones in! Sat up there in broad daylight, listening to music, having the time of his life. So I rang the oul fella on the mobile and told him come out quick, there's a fella in the yard , and that's when he turned around and saw me. He was down in a flash, that length of rebar there in his hand –' Bubbles nodded at the piece of metal in the grass '– and before I knew it he'd hit me a clout on the head.'

'I came into the yard and that's what I saw,' Creedon said. 'This fella stood over my son with a steel bar in his hand and my son's head pumping blood. To see your child like that, the shock of it.'

Noonan looked back towards the yard.

'What then? He made a run for it?'

'I shouted at him to stop, I just wanted him to stop,' Creedon said, shaking his head. 'But everything happened so quick.'

'Looks to me like he made a run for it, got as far as here –' Noonan indicated the flattened patch of grass Judge had been lying on '– turned back to face you, and then took the shot to his guts. Does that sound right?'

Creedon shook his head.

'It was a warning shot. A shot to scare him off.'

'Dad,' Bubbles said.

'You're telling me you weren't aiming for him?' Noonan said.

'I swear on my life I was not!' Creedon said.

'You took an awful fucking chunk out of him for a fella you weren't aiming for.'

'He was the one came here,' Creedon said. 'He came here!'

'Dad,' Bubbles repeated. 'Don't say nothing more.'

'You'll be saying plenty more, both of you,' Crean said. He unclipped a pair of handcuffs from his belt and sprung them open.

'Garda Swift,' he said, 'can you please place these on Mr Creedon.'

'I will come willingly,' Creedon said.

'This is how we're doing it, Mr Creedon,' Crean said as Swift took the cuffs from him. 'There's a team on the way and once this scene's secured we're going to run you and your son here down to the station and get everything on record. The cuffs are for your own security. Pronsius, you can do him from the front.'

Swift drew Creedon's arms together in front of his waist and clicked on the cuffs.

'Come here,' Crean said to Noonan, walking a dozen paces off into the field, still tentative on his ankle. She followed.

Dennis Crean was forty-nine years old to Noonan's forty-five. He had made Sergeant eighteen months ahead of her – later in his career relative to her, but before her, chronologically – and so, by the dictates of the informal but binding hierarchy that exists inside any official hierarchy, Crean was considered her superior, despite them sharing the same rank. Nobody had ever put it that way to her – nobody had ever had to, least of all Crean, who was impeccable in his behaviour towards Noonan. He was always careful to solicit her opinion and, often, to defer to her judgement. He gave her any amount of latitude and agency in her duties. But still, Noonan could never quite forget that that latitude and agency were only ever granted, and only ever his to grant. Noonan knew it, Crean knew it. She had made her peace with this arrangement a long time ago, and she tried not to hold it against Crean. If it wasn't him, it'd just be another fella, and probably one less considerate. Crean was reliable, decisive and loyal. He was a good policeman.

'How's the ankle?' Noonan asked him.

'I'll live. Are you OK?'

Noonan took off her cap. Navy, with the gold badge of the Garda crest set into the black band above the peak. Noonan rotated the cap in her hands and placed it back on her head.

'It's been a long weekend,' she said.

Crean was gazing off down the field.

'They're very presentable all the same, aren't they?' he said, nodding at the Ox Mountains.

'They are.'

'That's the thing about Mayo. I find it's very presentable from a distance. It's only up close it lets you down.'

Noonan managed a smile.

'The family will need to be told,' Crean said. 'Can you handle that?'

Noonan nodded.

Crean studied her for a moment, rooted out a pack of disposable tissues and offered the pack to her. He tapped his temple.

'Your forehead,' he said. 'You can't be showing up to the family's door with that poor fucker's blood all over your face.'

The forensics team arrived, as did Inspectors Burke and McElroy over from Castlebar. Crean and the inspectors escorted the Creedon men to Ballina station. Noonan and Swift detoured back to the station so that Noonan could clean up, change shirts and double-check the address they had on file. Noonan rang the listed number for Amy Mullally but got no answer and decided against leaving a message. She rang home, told Trevor she would be late.

'How are you now?' Noonan asked Swift as they idled in traffic in the town centre.

'I'm OK,' he said. 'I mean, you know.'

He did not complete the thought, smiling dumbly and gazing out at the streets of Ballina as if he weren't quite sure they were there. It was darker now, the street lights throwing down their harsh yellow dazzle.

'That the first death you seen on the job?' Noonan asked him.

'It's not been called yet.'

'No. But was it?'

'There was that young lad topped himself in the shed in Easky last Christmas.'

'I mean a killing.'

'There was a couple of gangland shootings up in Dublin, after I'd just got out of Templemore. Only saw the aftermaths, though. Never saw a fella dying in front of me like that. You?'

Noonan shook her head.

They were waiting on a light near the entrance to the Tesco carpark. A pack of teenage boys were crossing the road. There were five of them, moving in addled formation. They were dressed interchangeably in branded hoodies, some in tracksuit bottoms, some in jeans. They were clean-faced and dark-haired. They so resembled one another, at least at a passing glance, that they might all have been brothers. As they moved from street light to street light Noonan watched their bobbing, intent, vociferating heads and smiled, because the thing about boys was that they only had the one haircut. That haircut changed every couple of years, but whatever it was, they all had it. Noonan remembered that for a while – ten, twelve, fifteen years ago? – it had been the peroxide-blond highlights; every strutting little gangster coming up had the peroxide-blond highlights. The style now in vogue was tight at the sides, with just enough hair on top to brush forward or into a part. Her own sons wore that style, and each of these boys did too. For an idle moment Noonan's attention dwelled on the lad trailing the group, actually the tallest but not carrying himself that way, head hung and shoulders stooped, sunk in his thoughts it seemed, indifferent to the animated cross-talk of the four in front. He looked up and caught Noonan's eye. Without thinking, Noonan raised two fingers from the steering wheel in that ubiquitous gesture of laconic country salute.

The boy's neutral face compressed into a sudden snarl as he hocked a thick pearl of phlegm into the gutter by the squad car and kept on walking.

'Did you see that?' Noonan said to Swift, watching the boys recede in the rear-view mirror.

'See what?' Swift mumbled.

Noonan swerved the squad car on to the kerb, unclipped her seat belt and bolted out on to the pavement. She came right up behind the boy, grabbed a fistful of his collar and shoved him against the car park wall so forcefully her cap went twirling to the ground.

'What was that now? Have you something you want to say?' Noonan roared into the boy's face.

The boy looked at her, startled, a muscle jumping in his clenched jaw.

'Hey, he didn't do nothing,' one of his friends blurted.

'Shut up,' Swift said to the friend as he arrived on the scene.

'Well?' Noonan asked the boy.

'Tell me what I did,' the boy said.

'You know what you did!'

The boy said nothing. The muscle in his jaw stopped jumping.

'Pick that cap up,' Noonan said.

The boy looked at the Garda cap on the ground, looked back at Noonan.

'Pick. It. Up.'

Noonan released him from her grip and the boy reached down and picked up the cap. As she snatched it from his hand, he skittered out of her reach and straightened his rumpled top.

'You can't just be grabbing people for no reason,' he said.

Noonan looked at Swift, the boy's friends. She stepped up to the boy.

'You know well what you did,' she said. 'And you know *I* know. Have some fucking respect for yourself.'

She put her cap back on, nodded at Swift and turned on her heel.

'What the hell was that about?' Swift asked when they were back in the car.

'Let's get this done,' she said, putting the car into gear.

There was a large oval green at the centre of the Glen Gardens estate. Several teenagers were punting a ball around beneath the lunar glow of the park lamps, and a couple more were sprawled in the grass spectating, a little nest of bags and soft-drink bottles next to them.

'See that,' Noonan said. 'Any money there's drink in them bottles.'

'Want to go ruin their night?' Swift asked.

'Tonight, they're off the hook.' Once they'd persuaded Amy Mullally to let them come in, Noonan got a glimpse inside the sitting room as they passed down the hall. It was bathed in the glow of a TV, and the little girl, longer-limbed now, was curled in a chair staring at an iPad. Mullally brought them through to the kitchen. She was still perilously skinny, her hair up in a pineapple, the tendons in her neck flexing like high-tension wires when she spoke. Noonan gave a careful, broad outline of the events at the farm: Judge's apparent scheme to rob the oil tank, the residents confronting him. She said he had been shot and was not any more explicit about his injuries beyond describing them as extremely serious. This time, Amy Mullally did not shout or rant. She absorbed what Noonan told her without interruption. She did not debate or refute the narrative Noonan laid out. All she asked was if Dylan was going to die. Noonan reiterated that he had been taken to Castlebar General, and that that was all they could tell her as of right now.

Noonan and Swift stayed put while Mullally rang her mother, who came over to look after the daughter. Mullally agreed to let Swift accompany her to the hospital.

Back at the station the inspectors' unmarked Focus was parked out front. Noonan picked up the cafetière from her desk and brought it into the station's poky little kitchen. Crean was in there, mugs laid out on the counter, meditatively watching the kettle rattle to a boil.

'Castlebar's finest in with those two?' Noonan asked.

Crean came out of his thoughts, cracked a faint smile.

'They have me fetching the tea while they work their magic,' he said, pouring the water from the kettle into the mugs. 'Did you talk to the family?'

'The girlfriend. Swift is gone with her to Castlebar General.'

'The two will want your report the second it's done.'

'I'm getting to that right now,' she said, waving the cafetière at him.

Crean stood back so that Noonan could access the counter. He watched her refill the kettle, rinse out the cafetière and dump in a couple of spoonfuls of instant coffee.

'You know there's bags of beans you can get for that thing,' he said. 'Ground, whole, vanilla, real fancy stuff.'

'I know. I see them every time I'm at Tesco.'

'And you never bother with them?'

Noonan considered the cafetière, its chipped silver handle and scratched glass body. It was Trevor had bought it for her years ago, under the characteristically generous misapprehension it might inspire in her an enthusiasm for something more than the cheapest of cheap coffee.

'I just never got around to it. Every time I see the fancy stuff in the supermarket I think, ah, next time, and the next time I think the same.'

'Word came back from the hospital,' Crean said.

'OK,' Noonan said.

'Judge was just out of surgery when I spoke to them. Doctors said it'll be touch and go the next couple of days, but it's looking like he might pull through.'

'Are you kidding me?'

'I am not.'

The kettle came to a boil. Noonan placed her tailbone against the lip of the counter.

'The fucker,' she said, relieved and appalled. 'Oh, the rotten little fucker.'

'I reckon you might just have saved that rotten little fucker's life.'

'Stop,' Noonan groaned. 'When we were over at the girlfriend's house, giving her the low-down, the whole time in the back of my head I kept thinking how Judge had just about done her the favour of her life, getting the guts shot out of himself.'

'My condolences on his survival.'

'Only I was sure he was a goner.'

'So was I when I saw the state he was in. But as of right

now, Dylan Judge remains in the land of the living, thanks to you.'

'Thanks to me,' Noonan said with a shake of her head.

She filled the cafetière with hot water and brought it back to her desk. She knew the report would take her some time. She had a method, more time-consuming than strictly necessary, but it allowed her to be thorough. First she would get down, by hand, the most crucial details in order of their occurrence then she would go back and flesh those details out on the computer. She sat down and opened her notebook, reread the litter of harried notes she'd jotted down over the course of Bertie Creedon initial phone call.

*shoot*

*1 man*

*berty creedn*

*rathrdn*

*mlls trn*

*3 left*

*yello h*

*'92 fiat*

*son*

*1 shot*

*dbl brrl*

*bleed*

She poured a coffee, turned her notebook to a clean page and began to write.

# THE WAYS

THE LANDLINE was mewling again in the kitchen, obliging Pell Munnelly, woke now for good, to climb from the cosy rut of her bed and pad downstairs in bare feet. She skimmed her fingertips along the dulled grey-and-lilac grain of the walls, swatted each light switch she passed to feel less alone.

On the phone was the secretary from her little brother Gerry's school. The secretary was named Lorna Dawes, a pretty blonde sap Pell sometimes saw around town. Another fight, Sap said: Gerry and two lads in the basement locker rooms before first class, an argument escalating to blows. Now Gerry was being detained in Sap's office until such time as someone could come pick him up.

The receiver was hot against Pell's ear. There was snow in the back garden, a radiant pelt of the stuff with dark, snub-bodied birds dabbing across it. She lifted a foot from the lino, pressed her toes into the flannelled warmth of her standing calf.

'So who will I say is coming in?' Sap asked.

'Well, guess that'd be me,' Pell said.

Upstairs, she raked sleep knots and static electricity from her hair. She threw on three layers and an old combat jacket of Nick's, salvaged a knitted hat malodorous with scalp sweat from the boiler room, and slammed the front door. The snow in the concrete courtyard was still faintly cut with the tread-mark arcs of Nick's departed Vectra. Nick lived here in as small a way as he could. He was gone by first light and did not come back until near midnight. But he was the eldest, twenty-five and the state-sanctioned boss ever since the folks died off of cancer over consecutive summers, the mammy three years back, the daddy the year before last. Pell rang Nick on her mobile, counted to eight while the line rang out as she knew it would, sent a text. Then a second, more considered text: said not to worry, she'd bail the lump out herself.

Transport was a problem. Pell's breath smoked in the air. A horse, a runty juvenile skewbald, gawped at her from the field next to the house and flicked its filthy tail.

'You are no candidate,' Pell said.

A field further on was Swanlon's bungalow, the Munnellys' nearest neighbour. Pell discerned a bloom of chimney smoke, faint as a watermark against the white sky. Swanlon was a pensioner with a metal hip, his only earthly companion the rowdy black bitch of a Border collie he doted upon. Pell knew she could sweet-talk Swanlon into giving her a lift, though he would insist on bringing the dog, which he permitted to ride in the front passenger seat, having successfully conditioned the beast to wear a seat belt. But Pell's impression was that driving had lately become a fretful ordeal for the old man. Besides, Gerry would go spare if Swanlon's rusting wreck of a car, parping cloudlets of straw and dung out the exhaust, came up the school drive to collect him.

So Pell walked the quarter mile out to the main road. Town was seven miles away. She skirted the barbed spokes of the briars clustered along the road's verge. Across the fields, a row of pylons curved away into the haze. After a while, she heard a vehicle, turned to see a county bus approaching. She stepped into the middle of the road and started waving. The bus heaved to a halt. The driver, Mack Reddin, tut-tutted as Pell stamped her boots in the stairwell and thumbed her mam's expired bus pass from her wallet.

'You look like a cooked prawn, Pell,' Reddin said.

There were three elderly women on board. They smelled like the inside of kettles. Pell sat away from them. The warm bus wended through the countryside and Pell drowsed in her seat, her drooping forehead scuffing the wet window and starting her back awake.

In Swinford, Pell watched a skinny dark girl in a leather jacket and wool hat bunch an infant to her chest and attempt to collapse, one-handed, an uncollapsing stroller before tossing the thing, splayed and sideways, into the bus's undercompartment.

In Foxford, three lads got on, schoolboys. Pell was sixteen, and they were about the same. They shambled down the aisle, jackets open and school ties wrenched loose, at this hour brazenly on the doss. Boys interested Pell. They were what she missed most about school, watching them and being among them. She liked their creaturely excitability, their insistence, in one another's company, on shouting almost everything, almost all the time. She liked their unwieldy bodies – their hands like hammers and their loaflike feet, the way their Adam's apples beat like the chests of trapped birds when they talked at her. *At*, not *to*. Pell had already deciphered the difference: most lads were too afraid to talk to her, and instead just blustered into her vicinity.

There were also the boys who barely spoke at all, and these were the ones Pell liked best; the lads who were lean, with long arms and intricately veined wrists, who could stand to inhabit a silence for three seconds in a row. Steven Davitt, the lad at the rear of this pack, was such a specimen. A comely six-foot string of piss, faintly stooped, with shale eyes darting beneath a matted heap of curly black fringe. He shied from looking her way, of course. In the middle was one of the Bruitt boys, the scanty lichen of an unthriving moustache clinging to his lip. Paddy Guthrie, out in front, was stubby and pink and loudly yammering without looking at the two in tow. He was the ringleader, the smart-mouth.

They passed her and slung themselves into seats a few rows behind. There was an interval of scuffling noises, snickering, a distinctly aired *cunt* or *bollocks* or *shudafagup*, followed by a bout of intensive communal muttering. Then a shunt and a rattle as a body cannoned into the frame of the seat immediately behind Pell's.

'Hey. Hey, you.' It was Guthrie. Pell smelled beer on his breath.

'Hey,' he said again.

'What?' Pell said.

'You're Nicky Munnelly's sister, yeah?'

Pell nodded.

'And Gerry, Gerry's sister, yeah?'

'Uh-huh.'

'Gerry's àll right, isn't he, a header, but good for a laugh in the end,' Guthrie said. 'And the fella Nick – what used they call him, the Prowler, yeah, back in the day? Me brother Joe came up with him, said he used to torment the priests in there something wicked, broke their hearts every second day. And shagged anything that moved around town.' Guthrie's face blinked at her. Pell watched his thin, bright lips pull apart.

'What do you mean, saying that about my brothers?' she said.

'Ah no, I *respect* the *fuck* out of them,' Guthrie said. 'But, like, they're a line of hellions, the lads out your way, in't they?'

'I never gave it much thought,' Pell said.

'Where you going?'

'Town.'

'No shit. Whereabouts and whyfor?'

'Where are you going?' Pell shot back. 'Why aren't you in school?'

'You know Davitt? His ma's away, so we were back in his place. There's all this drink in the shed. Davitt's ma, she don't mind us having a couple the odd weekend, but we sneak a few extra now and then on the sly, in between, like this morning.' He licked his lips again. 'Bit of a buzz on, and now we're, well, we're heading back to school for the afternoon. Dossing gets boring, you know, trying to come up with stuff to actually fucking do.'

'You were on the doss, and now you're heading back into school?'

'Correct,' Guthrie said. 'For PE and art class. Handy

numbers. Ginty, the art teacher, lets us listen to music, long as we agree to "draw our feelings". A soft goon but an all-right one, Ginty. But, hey, you still out of school yourself like?'

Pell shrugged.

'Well for some, eh? You ever going to go back?'

The bus was in town now. Further along the quays, set behind a stone wall and a treeline, was the boys' school. Pell could see the slated peaks of the main building emerging from the crowns of the trees.

'It's where I'm headed right now,' Pell said, smiling, already bored with Guthrie.

Nick Munnelly was standing in an alley in the cold at the rear of the Bay Pearl Hotel, smoking and picking at the threads, the linty specks, snarled in the hairs of his forearm. It was something to do. Against the opposite wall of the alley was a skip brimming with bin bags. On the cobbled ground were crushed Styrofoam cups, plastic baggeens, and shreds of newspaper so snow-sodden they did not stir in the wind. Nick cuffed a boot heel against the doorway's concrete step. The side of his face was rashing into numbness. He was in a T-shirt and a spattered apron. He worked in the hotel kitchen, a muggy, frantic space where the staff sweated through shifts stripped to single layers. The other smokers took their breaks inside, huddled beneath the grille of a ventilation shaft in an old storage room. Nick preferred the open alley, with its ripe rankness and keening draught. The cold was a pleasure to him because he could remove himself from its effect at any moment. But not yet: the true pleasure of relief, like any pleasure, was in its anticipation.

Being able to go inside afterwards would be better than having stayed inside in the first place.

Sean the Chinaman poked his head out the door.

'Jaysus, lad, it's nippy,' Sean said.

Nick said nothing.

'Your kids are here.'

Nick looked at Sean.

'Boy and a girl?'

'Yeah,' Sean said. 'A boy and a girl.'

Sean's actual name was Heng Chen. He changed it because Irish people couldn't handle the pronunciation. This mildly incensed Nick. Any grown human who couldn't manage Heng even, just Heng, after a few sincere attempts was being a purposefully ignorant fuck. Nick tried to explain this to Sean, but Sean, diplomatic as the woefully outnumbered must always be, said that he was happy to go with Sean. It was what some people did when they came over, he said, picked a native name. A Chinaman called Sean. It was funny, Nick thought, or maybe it wasn't.

'Nick?'

Nick shook his head and smiled. 'That's my bro and sis, you daft cunt. What age do I look?'

They were in the lounge, weather dripping from their jackets on to the shitty carpet. It needed replacing, but so did everything. The hotel was dying on its hole. Nick told them to sit, and they each took a leather chair by the street window. The chairs were too big for them, the leather creaky with disuse. Gerry climbed on to the chair on his hands and knees like a dog before righting himself in the squeaking seat. He had a gunked lip, a yellow plume on his cheek, a nostril rimmed with crusting red.

Nick looked at his little brother.

'Stop being a fucking prick,' he said.

Gerry slumped down. Nick saw that he was dazed. The adrenaline churned up by the fight had all ebbed away. Nick remembered the feeling; the rinsed muscles, the warm quiver of shot nerves. There was no point interrogating Gerry as to what had happened, or why. It didn't matter. Someday, someone was going to beat sense into the little shit, and Nick knew only that it was not going to be him.

'I was flat out here,' Nick said.

Pell dabbed at her wet nose with the cuff of her, no – it was Nick's combat jacket.

'I know,' she said.

'You know what I'm like with the fucking phone. But next time give them my number.'

'You're not going to answer.'

'No. But let that be those cunts' problem. That's what they're paid for.'

Nick glanced at the bar clock.

'Sean, be a doll and get the kitchen to fix this pair – what you want? Chips, burgers?'

'Curry chips and a quarter-pounder with cheese,' Gerry said immediately.

'Pell?'

Pell was looking out the window.

'The same.'

'My lunch ain't due till three, but I can probably clear out before that,' Nick said. 'Eat that shit first and I'll drop you home.'

Nick went back through the kitchen and out again into the alley. There had been a minute left on his smoke break, and, with the sensation of tears boiling behind his eyes, he smoked that minute out.

'Bambi on ice,' Nick said.

He was driving, Pell up front beside him. Gerry was in the back, asleep, or feigning it. All the morning's excitability over, the little wanker was enjoying the bonus of having the afternoon off and the additional impending idleness of however many days of suspension the school decided to slap him with. Pell was brooding, chin tucked into her shoulder, eyes fixed out her window.

On the way to the car, she'd stepped off the pavement and gone down on her arse on the ice. Gerry, in his post-scrap stupor, had come to life, clapping and chanting, 'Get up, Pell, get up, Pell,' as she rocked back and forth. Nick had let this performance go for thirty seconds before lifting a boot and, glancing Gerry's knee, sending him clattering against the bonnet of a nearby car. Nick had not offered Pell a hand, because Pell would not have taken an offered hand. Instead, he'd grabbed her under her armpits and hauled her to her feet. 'Leggo,' she'd growled.

Nick watched the road. It was disorienting to be away from work at this hour. The afternoon sky was swamped with clouds, and the glare made the linings of his eyelids ache, all that dazzle piled to the low brink of the horizon.

'Bambi on ice,' he said again.

Pell acted tough. She was a bunched slip of a thing with a mouth that got vicious real fast. With her hackles up, she was liable to go for anyone. Whenever she came out with an exceptionally cutting remark, Nick wanted to take her in his arms and tell her, *Your mammy and your daddy would be so proud.*

'Don't be sulking, Bambi,' Nick said, laughing, and went to pet her brow.

'Prick off,' Pell said, and swung at his shoulder.

Without taking his eyes off the road, Nick grabbed her wrist and turned her limb towards her until he had Pell's head pinned to the passenger window. Pell had a tiny fucking head for a sixteen-year-old human, Nick thought, and laughed as he felt its diminutive shape vibrate where it was trapped. Her free hand slapped at his braced arm. But up until he relinquished his grip – he wasn't hurting her – Pell's jaw remained taut, and she fumed through her nose but said no word, refused to beg to be let go.

He slowed the car to a crawl in the yard, arced around, and, without waiting for the Vectra to come to a stop, the two opened their doors and timed their leaps clear. He completed the circle, watched them in the mirror. He bipped the horn. Neither looked back at him.

Swanlon and his dog were standing at the gate of his house. Swanlon put out a claw, held it there. Nick pulled up.

'How's young Munnelly?' Swanlon said, his nostrils plugged with silvery, unkempt hair.

'Sound. You?'

The old man snorted, spat.

'You not in work?'

'Heading straight that way now. Had to drop that pair back.'

'Young Gerry not in school?'

'School's not an arrangement he's enthralled with just now.'

'The scholarly burdens,' Swanlon said. 'He's a good lad, but.'

'He is,' Nick said. 'When he's asleep.'

Swanlon grubbed at the springy cartilage of the dog's ear. He'd inherited the farm from his oul fella, decades back, had worked it here in tandem with his mother until she, too, died off. As far as Nick knew, Swanlon had never gone anywhere or done anything beyond tending to his acres. He was just an ailing, ancient sham who knew almost nothing about life.

'And what about young Pell?' Swanlon continued.

Nick ground his teeth. 'What about her?'

'I saw her stalking straight out that road this morning, head up. Looked like a soldier making off to war.'

'That's how she always looks.'

'She should finish her schooling, too. She's a sharp tack.'

'I know, I know. But, the way I see it, that's up to her.'

Pell had been out of school for almost two months now. She'd started junior-cert year right after the da's funeral. She hadn't missed a day that Nick could recall, was eerily compliant through the year, then failed every single exam. This year, she was supposed to repeat, but when school started, back in September, she would not get out of bed. Just would not get out of bed. The third day, Nick, sick of appealing, barged into her room, grabbed her by the ankles, and began to walk backwards. Pell, on her back, did not resist. She held his gaze and needed three stitches in her head where she'd hit the floor.

'Ah, I know, but still,' Swanlon said. He shifted his gaze. 'You up to your eyes in the job?'

'Not particularly,' Nick said.

'You're hardly about.'

Nick squinted. 'You keeping tabs?'

Swanlon smiled. 'Not in an especial way. But what else have I to be doing?'

Nick looked up at Swanlon. 'I don't know. I couldn't imagine. There's not so much as a square inch spare inside my head to ponder what it is you'd have to be doing with your time.'

'All right,' Swanlon said.

Nick angled his arm out the window. He watched the dog raise its gleaming snout to his palm.

'Dogs always look sorry for something,' he said.

Gerry dismounted, hitched his horse to the post outside the Monteroy Saloon, and cycled through his weapons inventory, topping up the ammo in his twin revolvers and his Winchester repeater. The stars were out. Pianola notes drifted from the saloon's double doors. Civilians walked the edges of the wide dirt street with their eyes on their shoes. Cicadas, crickets, whatever they were, ticked way out in the desert dark.

Gerry, the flesh-and-guts boy, was lumped on his bean-bag, the only light in his room the glow from the TV atop the dresser. His PlayStation wheezed on the floor at his slippered feet. The game was Blood Dusk 2. You played as Cole Skuse, an ex-Yankee soldier and mercenary. Right now, Gerry was about to attempt the rescue of Skuse's love interest, a beautiful blonde prostitute named Dora Levigne. She was being held hostage by the Cullen gang inside the saloon. Mission objective was get in there, ventilate as many of the Cullen boys as possible, and get her out. The Cullen faction was part of a larger horde of roving rapists, murderers, thieves and scalp hunters led by a scarred brute known only as the Padre. The Padre was your true and final adversary, the man who, in the game's prologue, had ordered the murder of your family.

Gerry liked Blood Dusk 2, but was becoming less and less enamoured of the repetitious, shootout-intensive missions you were obliged to complete in order to advance the plot. The game weighed things too much in your favour. You had unlimited lives, too many automatic save points, too nuanced and forgiving a targeting system for taking out your opponents. What was worth it, what kept Gerry coming back, was the game map. The map was gorgeous, two hundred square miles of simulated, fully interactable nineteenth-century North American frontier. While the missions tended to cluster in the towns and settlements that occupied only a small percentage of the game's physical environment, Gerry had spent countless hours ranging through the enormous remainder of the map. He had discovered the remnants of Indian graves, chased down buffalo on an open plain, drunk moonshine with a benignly deranged prospector by the shore of a moonlit creek. The landscape teemed with wildlife and, to a lesser extent, other people, and you could, of course, shoot every living thing in the game, though Gerry refrained whenever possible. At sunset, he would goad his nag up the trail of a hill to watch the sinking rays cut across the cliff walls of a distant canyon, the ponderous flecks of vultures lagging in the thermals, circling something dying unseen on the canyon floor . . .

'Shhtburk.'

'Hah?' Gerry said.

'Shit. Brick,' Pell repeated from the doorway, looking down at Gerry. She was in Uggs and sweatpants, holding a glass with a clear liquid in it. Pell liked vodka, liked to lingeringly nurse thimblefuls of the stuff in the evening. Off school, and drinking when she liked: Pell had Nick under her thumb. The funny thing was that Nick, back before the folks croaked, had been mad for drinking, going out, and the general pursuit of hell-raising. Now he'd turned brutally sensible: worked every hour he could, stayed diligently sober, did not even bother with women any more.

'Yeah?' Gerry said.

'I've made chops. Potatoes and a tiny, tiny little bit of veg, so we don't all get scurvy. Will you have some, please?'

'Not hungry,' he said, though he was, but somewhere amid the clutter of his room there was a half-full, party-sized tub of Pringles, likely still perfectly edible, that would do.

'How's the face?'

Gerry shrugged, licked his lips. His saline made the tenderness of his split lip buzz.

'Who'd you set on this time?' Pell said. 'Or who was it set on you?'

Keith Timlin. Now, Keith Timlin was a mate, but, like all of Gerry's mates, the friendship was susceptible to these eruptions, and afterwards Gerry could never work out whose fault it was, or account for the rapidity with which the mood had escalated from idle chat to banter to mock-slagging and then to real, aggressive slagging. But Gerry liked Timlin! Gerry liked Timlin more than most! Certainly more than Shaughnessy, who all of a sudden had waded in on Timlin's side and started sneering about the smell coming off Gerry. It was Shaughnessy who only a couple of weeks back had been getting reams of slagging mileage out of making fun of Timlin's special shoe he had to wear on account of having unevenly long legs (the 'clopper', as Shaughnessy called it) and of Timlin's admittedly ratty-looking features, his pinched snout and poky teeth. Gerry had been the one sticking up for Timlin then.

'Brendan Shaughnessy,' Gerry said.

'There were two, though; your one Dawes said there was another lad involved. Was the other lad fighting you, too, or sticking up for you, or what?'

'The other lad was with Shaughnessy. They were both against me.'

'And did you start it?'

Gerry said nothing.

'I'll take that as a yeah.'

Gerry loathed being on exhibit like this, down on his fat arse, Pell looming above him. On the screen, the cowboy Skuse idled in the street and kicked mindlessly at dirt clods, setting the spurs of his boots chiming. Gerry kept looking at the screen.

'You can't keep at that, Gerry,' Pell said. 'Being an idiot.'

'School is packed with dickheads.'

'The world is packed with dickheads,' Pell said. 'You've got to stop rising to them.'

'I will,' Gerry said, just to get her to shut up.

'You won't,' she replied.

'I will. I will soon.'

Gerry said nothing else, just waited until Pell slid from the doorway, then sprang up, banged the door, and returned to his beanbag. He grazed the 'X' button with his thumb, and Skuse drew his pistol and braced into a firing stance. He strode into the Monteroy Saloon and blew away everything that moved.

It got late. Gerry found the tub of Pringles and finished them off. The house quietened. Pell didn't bother him again, and Gerry kept playing. Eventually, he heard a car. From his window, he could see that the yard light had come on. He stood up to look. The door of Nick's Vectra was open, as was the boot. The car, parked at an untidy diagonal to the house, looked abandoned, ambushed. It was empty inside, welling with shadows. The yard light made the snow around the car unnaturally bright. Then his brother appeared, returning from the direction of the house's front door. Gerry watched Nick, still in his white T-shirt and white work trousers, his breath trailing visibly from his mouth. Even the canvas sneakers he was wearing were white. Nick was drawing shopping bags from the boot. He must have been freezing, his shoes soaked. A wince flickered across Gerry's features as he considered the lengthy detour his older brother would have had to make in order to accommodate so late a run for provisions: the 24-hour petrol station on the Dublin road was the only place open this side of midnight, and it was five miles out the other side of town. He wished he liked his giant humourless prick of a brother more.

Gerry heard shouts, gunfire, and turned back to the screen. He had forgotten to pause the game, and Skuse was taking hits. Dora Levigne had long been rescued and returned to the care of her madam, and Gerry, travelling onward from Monteroy to the northern town of Aristo, had meandered into a forested area, where he'd stumbled upon

a Cullen encampment set into a treed thicket at the foot
of a hill. Gerry had left Skuse crouched behind a wedge of
rock in preparation for an assault, but now a number of the
Cullen party had manoeuvred behind him and were unloading their weapons into Skuse's back. Gerry turned his avatar
just in time to take a fatal shot to the torso, and the screen
cut to black. In the black, words appeared:

DO YOU WISH TO CONTINUE?

YES / NO.

Gerry growled. The game was so easy, it enraged him to
die this cheaply. He felt like throwing the pad through the
TV. He shut his eyes and breathed in, heard noises downstairs. He stepped over to the closed door. They were in the
kitchen, Nick and Pell. Gerry had figured that Pell was in
bed by now, but no, she'd either just gone back down or had
been down there all this time. They were talking, though
their voices were too faint and muffled to comprehend.
Gerry got down on to his knees and pressed his face into
the rancid fuzz of the carpet, the better to get his ear up to the
half-inch horizontal gap between his door and the floor. He
held his breath but still could not make out what they were
saying. Nor could he reliably gauge their tone. He wondered, as all eavesdroppers do, if he was the subject under
discussion: wee indolent tubs sitting on his hole upstairs
and refusing to come out of his room. It might be something they could laugh about together, at least.

There was a game Gerry liked to play, and he realised
that he was playing it now: in his head, the muffled voices
of his brother and his sister became the voices of his folks.
It helped that he could barely recall what their voices had
sounded like. The folks were growing vague to him.

Sometimes, in the street, he would break out in a sweat as he registered, in the corner of his eye, the particular lanky stride of a man or the way a woman paused to slip the strap of a bag off her shoulder and rummage around for something, but then he'd look and, with a pang of utter relief, realise that there was no resemblance at all. With his parents safely dead, it was safe to imagine that they were not, and so he imagined descending the stairs, strolling in on not just Pell and Nick but the folks – the daddy unwizened, the mammy unwigged – seated at the kitchen table, grinning and abashed after their long and flagrant absence. They would look at Gerry and, in low, sincere voices he would instantly know as theirs, say, 'Sorry for dying, son.'

And Gerry would say, 'That's OK.' Gladdened, and made generous by their remorse, he would turn to Pell and Nick and say, 'Sorry for being an arsehole today, lads.' And Pell and Nick would say, 'That's OK, Gerry. We're sorry for being arsehole, too.'

The fibres of the carpet pricked like tiny, finite flames against his face. After a while he had to get up, to relieve the pressure building between his temples. Gerry stood, and, as the blood descended from his head, flurries of bright-yellow and purple spots multiplied in the dark in front of his eyes. Five minutes ago, he had felt exhausted, ripe only for the pillow, but now he was electrically wakeful. He held the pad in his hand and watched the blinking spots fade away. In the dark, on the screen, the question remained.

DO YOU WISH TO CONTINUE?

# THE ALPS

A Hitachi Hiace with piebald panelling, singing suspension and a reg from the last millennium rolled into the car park of the Swinford Gaels football club late on a Friday evening. The Hiace belonged to Rory Hughes, the eldest of the three brothers known as the Alps, and the Alps travelled everywhere together in it. The brothers stepped out and, with a decisive slam of the van's side door, moved off across the moonscape of the car park in the order of their conceptions, Rory on point, the middle brother Eustace close behind, and the youngest, Bimbo, in dawdling tow.

The Alps, weary after a week of work, did not speak. They listened to the chunked slippage of the gravel under their workboots. On the floodlit pitch a pheasant groomed itself beneath the sagging diagonals of the goalmouth netting. The night air was close and cloudless, sultry with the stink of silage coming off the surrounding fields.

Asleep almost on his feet, Bimbo noticed a light moving up in the sky. A shining point, minuscule as a star or a transatlantic plane, but moving far too nimbly and erratically to be either. Bimbo roused. He watched the point descend at an angle, shoot back up at ninety degrees, then stop and wobble in place. A spaceship, Bimbo fancifully thought, for the point's motion, however clumsy, seemed purposeful. Then Bimbo noted the patch of land the pip of light was bobbing above and figured it out.

'See that,' he said.

'Hah?' grunted Eustace.

'What I'm looking at,' said Bimbo. His older brothers turned to Bimbo, then faced back in the direction he was looking.

'Which would be?' said Rory.

'See,' said Bimbo, focusing his attention on the point. As if by telepathy the older two duly clocked the light.

'What in the Christ is that when it's at home?' said Rory.

'It's a drone,' said Bimbo. 'Them acres over there belong to Marcus Landry, right? I heard he was sourcing the highest-spec drones he could get his hands on to keep track of his herds. He's rakes of livestock and animals and they do be regularly going missing on him,' Bimbo said. 'The surmise is some intrepid bollocks is poaching them.'

'That would be the surmise, all right,' said Rory.

'Drones,' said Eustace, 'would you be well?'

'Landry is a man of means,' said Rory. 'Men of means are rarely right in the head.'

'Drone surveillance,' said Bimbo. 'I think it's class.'

The Alps were shortish men with massive arses and brutally capable forearms. They breathed coltishly through their noses and rolled their shoulders with a circumspect flourish whenever women crossed their paths. They billed themselves as tradesmen, though between them had never acquired a qualification in any particular trade. What they did was try things at a competitive rate. They painted, wired, plumbed, tiled, but where they excelled was in the displacement of the earth: digging holes, filling holes back in. Holes of any circumference and depth. Holes were their forte.

Bimbo had just turned thirty-seven, Rory and Eustace were coming up on fifty. The Alps still felt young in their souls but it was the bloodshot eyes, pouched necks and capitulating hairlines of middle age that leered back at them from mirrors. They ate too much takeaway, slept fitfully, downed vats of Guinness every weekend. In addition to their remorseless lifestyles there was the disgraceful odds offered by their genes. The Alp family tree was a stump mutilated by cancer and coronaries. Few of their male forebears had made it into their sixties, which meant the Alps' days were probably almost over. The Alps carried this knowledge around with them. Because what else could they do but carry it. They were gleeful, boisterous and deprecating in company, except when they weren't. Then, it was like a switch got switched. It was not true to say any of them had a temper, only that they possessed a reserve of a certain kind of energy, an energy that periodically required venting. Fights happened and they got in them. The outcomes, generally in their favour, were nonetheless irrelevant. The Alps were built for punishment, they were not built to last.

The brothers came through the clubhouse door to a mild effusion of hollers and hellos from the handful of patrons already ensconced. There was the teenage barman Mikey Reilly with his pink cheeks and sawdust crew cut. There was Softly Broughan, recently retired half forward for the county senior football team, dubbed Softly for his loping running style and ability to ghost between the opposition lines. Softly now managed his father's haulage company out of Westport. He was a vivid dresser and was tonight arrayed in a baronial waistcoat with fobbed pocket watch, cornflower neckerchief and a champagne bomber jacket of distressed leather. On the arm of Softly was not his fiancée, the solicitor Stella McIlenden, but one of Stella's younger sisters, Denise, a primary schoolteacher and finalist in the 2014 Mayo Rose of Tralee heats. The pensioner Peader Ginty was there with the tank of purified oxygen snugged into the tartan trolleybag he was obliged to wheel around with him everywhere, and his scowling daughter Moira, herself in her fifties, in the leather jacket and narrow black clerical trousers she favoured, the dark glasses she never took off on account of her chronic photophobia.

'Anyone clap eyes on that peacock outside beyont in the goals?' Bimbo asked.

'I did not,' Softly said, 'but in any case I'd wager that would very much be a pheasant you were looking at, Bimbo.'

Bimbo looked Softly up and down.

'You look like Kanye, kid,' Bimbo said.

'Kid, I am Kanye,' Softly said.

Rory and Eustace slid on to a pair of stools in front of the taps.

'How's the form, Mikey?' Rory said.

'The form remains legendary,' Mikey said, already working on their Guinnesses.

'A round of cheese toasties as well,' Rory said. 'We're running on fumes here.'

'Onions and mustard?' Mikey asked.

'Load them beasts up,' Rory said. 'And three packages of Tayto while you're at it.'

Mikey turned to the shelves behind him and the brothers regarded his neck, bright pink, savagely sunburnt.

'That's an awful scalded neck you have on you there, Mikey,' Eustace said.

'I was up on the roof of the mother's house listening to an MMA podcast this afternoon and didn't I only fall asleep,' Mikey said.

'Gutted for you,' Rory said.

Bimbo remained on his feet. He paced around the lounge, brooded at the burgundy carpet with its pattern of custard-coloured spades like the spades on playing cards, his hands dangling at his sides, limp as strangled game. He was antsy now because of the presence of Denise McIlenden. He could not remove her from his peripheral vision, nor did he want to. Her skin was an improbably deep and even brown and she was in jeans and heels and she smelled absolutely unreal. She was one of them ones who was already beautiful but trowelled on the cosmetics anyway and while there was a certain type of man who claimed he preferred natural-looking women Bimbo did not see how you could mind either way. The Alps were not men comfortably acquainted with the carnal, but they could become as fissured and rent with yearning as anyone.

Bimbo had done three sides of the room and was coming up past Moira and her wheezing daddy.

'What's it at?' Moira asked.

'What's what at?'

'The peacock. The pheasant. What's it at?'

'Oh now, just existing,' Bimbo said.

'Is that so,' she said. Moira had a big nose, scraggly hair, a perpetually pursed mouth. She was inclined to taciturnity anyways but the dark glasses made her expressions completely unreadable. Bimbo suspected she played up the photophobia in order to maintain precisely this effect. There was always a hint of mocking in her voice and Bimbo had no time for her, really: she reminded him of the rock and roll singer Bob Dylan and he had no time for Bob Dylan and his long-winded, tuneless stylings neither.

'And how are you, Peader?' he asked Moira's father.

Peader Ginty started. His face was bloated and yellow, the corners of his eyes sudsy with discharge. A nose cannula hooked over his ears fed him oxygen out of the tank nestling in his trolleybag. He was diabetic, could barely walk because of his gout, his heart was riddled with stents. He was by this stage of things a big watery bag of imperilled organs, and the only parts of him that still worked, worked because of ongoing medical intervention. Moira was stuck as his carer and if she was even a tiny bit more hospitable in her demeanour Bimbo would have felt sorry for her.

'Oh, good, now. Not bad now,' Peader wheezed. His breathing reminded Bimbo of the antiquated range in his granny's. 'And yourself, Bimbo?'

'Nothing worth complaining about.'

'People who have nothing to complain about lack character,' Moira said.

'Oh,' Bimbo said. 'Is that true? Peader, do you reckon that's true?'

'What?' Peader said.

'Go back to sleep,' Moira said.

'I'm not sleepy,' Peader said.

'Have you taken your pill, Daddy? You have to take your pill.'

'I do be always taking that pill. I never miss that pill.'

'Good man,' Bimbo said. 'You tell her.'

'Don't be getting him worked up,' Moira said.

'I do take them pills like clockwork,' Peader said.

Bimbo sighed. He tilted his head back, squared his shoulders. Denise McIlenden was behind him. He could smell her watching him.

'Peader,' Bimbo said. 'I'll race you round the car park. A single lap, full bore. Fella comes last owes the other ten bob.'

'I'd leave you for dust, kid,' Peader said.

'You would, too.'

'Come over here and eat your toastie before I do,' ordered Rory. Bimbo looked his brothers' way. Rory's mouth was shiny with grease, Eustace had his face down almost on the plate, the pair savaging at their food with the shameless avidity of children.

Bimbo came over, took his pint and crisps.

'You don't want that?' Rory nodded at the sandwich.

'Have at it.'

'I will, so,' Rory said, transferring the toastie on to his plate.

'Have you your Skybox fixed yet?' Eustace asked Mikey.

'We do.'

'Throw it on there.'

Mikey picked the remote off a back shelf, turned on the TV angled above the bar and began promptly flicking.

'Tell me when,' Mikey said.

'Please don't go turning up the telly,' Softly said.

'Why?' Bimbo said.

'TV lowers the tone,' Softly said.

'The *tone*?' Bimbo said.

'Before you boys barrelled in, we were sitting here in silence,' Softly said, 'and it was an awful *cultivated* silence.'

'I'd say it was,' Bimbo said. 'And oh, do you know what else I saw out there?'

'Aside from the peacock,' Moira said.

'Pheasant,' Softly said.

'You don't know for sure I didn't see a peacock,' Bimbo said.

'I will put down any money it wasn't a peacock,' Softly said.

'They are related creatures, though,' Denise said, 'so it's not like either of you are far wrong.'

'Thank you, Denise,' Bimbo said. He caught Softly's eye. 'I suppose they are awful easy creatures to get mixed up.'

'Not if you know what you're at,' Softly said.

'I saw a drone,' Bimbo announced, 'flitting about over Marcus Landry's fields.'

'A drone,' Peader said.

'It's like a little unmanned craft,' Bimbo said. 'A little spaceship job.'

'I heard talk about him at something like that, all right,' Softly said.

'Shush,' Eustace said, eyes intent on the telly. 'That'll do, Mikey.'

A playback of a women's track race was on. It was the jittery, in-between bit before the race, where the competitors go through their final warm-ups and rituals and dance nervously on the starting line like they had to use the toilet. Mikey kept the sound low.

Bimbo opened his packet of crisps and offered around

to the other patrons to no avail. He wondered what Softly and the younger McIlenden were playing at. It was an awful suggestible alignment they presented, though there was nothing anyone could say, because it could all be innocent. Softly loved himself, was the thing, and the Stella one was lovely, but then the Denise one was lovely too, and a normal man would be down on his knees with gratitude just to have the one or the other. But Softly was the type of fella would never settle just for satisfaction.

Bimbo spouted the foil pack and shook the last crumbs of crisp into his palm. He licked his thumb for the last of the salt. He glanced at Denise. She was staring unhappily at the TV, the fingertips of one hand absently resting on her neck.

'Back in a tick,' Bimbo muttered.

Bimbo stormed into the jacks, thrummed a sulphurous piss into the gurgling trough. On the wall above the urinal someone had written

AISLING MCILENDEN WONT U SUCK ME OFF
BEHIND YOUR DADDYS FODDER TROUGH

Bimbo tutted. Aisling was the third McIlenden sister, only in college still, and in Bimbo's estimation the least finest, but that was only relatively speaking. Aisling McIlenden was lovely and there was absolutely no call for such public traduction of her or indeed any other *beoir* on account of just being good-looking. Bimbo spat into his palm and tried rubbing the foul couplet away, but it was written in permanent marker. He ground the heel of his palm in a circle against the cool brick and even as he did so he felt his horn rouse in his other hand.

'Ah, now,' he said, disgusted at the impertinence of his body.

A trace of Denise McIlenden's scent had carried itself into the bleachy stench of the jacks, and it taunted Bimbo's nose and it went down into his body and it taunted him in his blood. Bimbo stepped into a stall, drew the latch. Forty-six seconds later he came back out and washed his hands in the sink.

When Bimbo returned to the lounge there was a young man sitting on the stool that would have been Bimbo's if Bimbo had taken a seat. The young man had the hunched, spidery posture of an adolescent, though his face looked older. He was dressed in black and he had a sword. Bimbo did not register the sword at first, because who expects a sword? The first thing he noticed was the silence that had settled over the other patrons, and for a humiliating moment he believed the silence was for him, that all present were somehow aware of what he had just perpetrated in the jacks.

The young man turned to Mikey.

'As I was saying.'

Then Bimbo registered the sword. The sword was sheathed in a scabbard and resting across the young man's knees, his hand nestled around the sword's long handle.

'You were saying you walked here,' Mikey said.

'I was saying it's a fair walk to here from all the way over beyont in Foxford,' the young man said.

Bimbo made his way over to the counter.

'It is a fair walk if you walked it, all right,' Bimbo said. It was eleven miles to Foxford and there were no street lights on the country road once you got out of the town and this kid was in dark clothing. He would not have made it this far without being run into the ditch a hundred times.

'This is Swinford I'm landed in,' the young man said.

'As near as makes no odds,' Bimbo said.

'It's just I'm not familiar,' the young man said. 'Swinford is to me a place you only ever pass through.'

'Let's go,' Denise McIlenden said to Softly, and stood up. Her eyes were wide and white. Everyone else had the half-lidded, deferred expressions of people who could not tell what it was they were looking at. He was just a young man. He had a sword. Bimbo could not believe it.

Denise picked her purse up from off the bar counter and flusteredly tugged the strap over her shoulder.

'What are you doing?' Softly asked.

'I'd like to go now is what I'd like,' Denise said.

'We have drinks,' Softly said.

'Well I am going.'

'No one should leave on my account, is what no one should do,' the young man said. He shifted on the stool and Bimbo's heart jumped. But the young man stayed seated.

Softly reached out and put his hand on Denise's forearm.

'Finish your drink,' he said.

'I don't want it.'

'Just sit. For five more minutes.'

'So did you say you're from Foxford?' Rory said to the young man.

'No.'

'But you said you just came from there, just now.'

'I know the place,' the young man said. 'My father lives that way. I should say used to live that way. There's a dry-out clinic there in Foxford, did you know that?'

'I did know that,' said Rory. 'I would know Foxford well, what there is of it to know. What has you all the way out this way?'

'None of your business,' the young man said.

'I was just being polite.'

'I don't think you were just being polite.'

'I think I was, as a matter of fact,' said Rory.

'Come here,' Eustace said to the young man. 'Do you want a drink?'

'I do not drink,' the young man said and swallowed. 'I mean I should not drink.'

'Says who, now?' Eustace said.

'It would be the general opinion held of me I should not drink.'

'That would be the general opinion held of most of us, I reckon,' Eustace said.

'When I was twelve,' Rory said, 'I pinned a Pioneer badge to my chest and forswore the taking of drink for all time. By the time I was thirteen I was lashing the stuff into me.'

'You have a weak will,' the young man said.

'That could certainly have been a factor,' Rory admitted.

'Do not be coming in here telling people they are weak-willed,' Denise said.

The young man looked at Denise.

'Are you a cat lady or a dog lady?' he said to her.

'Excuse me?' Denise said.

'Are you a cat lady? Or a dog lady?'

'Oh ho ho,' Bimbo said. 'This is one of them riddles.'

'How is it a riddle?' Eustace said. 'He's just asking for a preference.'

'It is a riddle,' Bimbo insisted. 'The choices are symbological. The dog is God in this equation. The dog is always God.'

'She's a dog lady,' Softly said to the young man.

'Good,' the young man said. 'I have always considered myself . . . a dog man.'

'What's the cat, so, in the equation?' Eustace asked Bimbo.

'Cats are awful eerie creatures,' the young man said, 'and they should never have been domesticated.'

'Will you settle now and have that drink?' Bimbo said to the young man.

'What are you drinking?' the young man asked, nodding at Bimbo's pint.

'This?'

'Yes. What is it?'

'It's a Guinness, lad,' Bimbo said with some incredulity. An Irishman not knowing what a Guinness was. It was like looking at a boot and not knowing what it was.

'Can I have one of them?'

'I suppose you can.'

'How many of them would you drink of a night?'

'Of a night? Well now, maybe . . . I would say . . . five, ten, whatever.'

'That's an awful lot.'

'It is, but sure don't I've an awful spacious build on me.'

'This fella,' Eustace said, nodding at the young man.

'This fella is unreal,' Rory said.

'Mikey, get this unreal young fella a Guinness,' Bimbo said.

'Aye,' Mikey said.

'I'm not going into rounds, though,' the young man said.

'Well, there's nobody here saying you have to do that,' Bimbo said.

'I know it's the convention. You buy me one, I buy you one back. But I'm not going into rounds. I can tell you that.'

'Good on you, young fella,' Moira said. 'The round mentality is an awful egregious one.'

'You have a sword,' Bimbo said to the young man.

The young man looked down at his lap.

'I do.'

'Why do you have a sword?'

'For protection.'

'Who do you need protecting from?'

'From my brothers.'

'Oh. How many brothers do you have?'

'Nine.'

'Nine?'

'Nine.'

'That's some collection of brothers to have in this day and age,' Bimbo said.

'So they tell me,' said the young man.

'And how many of these nine brothers want to hurt you, then?'

'Oh, just like—' The young man shifted without energy in his seat. 'I would say two or three of them.'

'And why do they want to hurt you?'

The young man blinked, swallowed. Mikey presented

him with his Guinness. The young man rotated the glass on the counter, and both he and Bimbo considered the cream head.

'That's some pour, Mikey,' Bimbo said. 'Head on it as neat as a hotel duvet.'

'By all accounts I don't endear myself to people in my actions or manner,' the young man said. 'So they tell me.'

'Even if that's true I doubt it merits going about the place with a sword, now, does it?' Bimbo said.

'It is a katana,' the young man said.

'Hah?' grunted Bimbo.

'Properly speaking, it is a katana blade,' the young man said. 'Arm of choice among the warrior class in feudal Japan.'

'A katana,' interjected Softly. 'That's what I thought, all right.'

'Well of course Softly knew it was a katana,' Bimbo said. 'Give him another minute and he'll be lecturing the lad on how he's holding it wrong.'

'Are we all right, Bimbo?' Softly said.

'Don't be telling the fella who's walked in off the Fox-ford road with a katana in his hand that you know more about his blade than he does,' Bimbo said.

'I'm not saying I know more than him,' retorted Softly. 'I'm just saying that I had in mind that the blade was a katana. Sure you'd need see only a couple of movies to know that.'

'I can't take this,' said Denise. She got back up off her stool.

'Sit down, D,' Softly said.

'To be accurate, it is a replica,' continued the young man. 'A high-end replica, but a replica all the same.'

'Can you run someone through with it?' said Bimbo.

'I. Am. Leaving,' Denise said.

'Leave so,' Softly said.

'You can,' said the young man. 'But it lacks the tensility, lightness and penetrative edge of a genuine katana. With a well-timed slash you could disembowel somebody no bother with the genuine article, but not so with a replica.'

'Are you handy with it anyway?' Bimbo said.

'My technique does need work,' the young man said.

'Will you show us?' Bimbo said.

'Please do not take out the sword,' Denise said.

'Yeah,' drawled Mikey. 'I don't think I can permit a drawn sword on the premises, lads.'

'Don't heed them, young fella,' Rory said.

'I mean we are definitely in dicey territory already,' Mikey said, 'just having a sword on the premises in the first instance.'

'It's a replica of a sword, not a sword itself,' Bimbo said.

'Fair point,' Eustace said.

'Would you require a licence for a sword?' Peader Ginty said.

'That's an awful good question, Daddy,' Moira said.

'Go on, buck,' Bimbo said. 'Get out on the floor and throw us a few samurai shapes.'

The young man, who was looking increasingly grave and agitated, took a long pull of his Guinness.

'Yucky,' he said.

'That's the stuff for you,' Rory said.

The young man stood up off his stool, strode into the middle of the lounge floor and smoothly drew the blade out of the scabbard. He raised the sword over his head and the contour of its curve flashed in the bar light. He braced his thighs, leaned to his left and whipped the blade down and back up in a clean arc, repeated the gesture on his right side.

'Jesus Christ,' Denise said.

'Fair play,' Bimbo said.

'Lads, seriously, I can't be sanctioning this,' Mikey said.

'We. Have. To. Go,' Denise said.

Softly, jaw clenched, got up off his stool and marched smartly to the clubhouse door. He fumbled in his jacket pocket, pulled out his car keys. Nudging open the door with his foot, he flung the keys out into the dark of the car park, then marched back to his stool and sat down.

'Go when you like so, D,' he said in a tight, low voice. 'Mikey, another pint.'

'Congratulations,' Denise said. 'Congratulations on thinking that one through. The joke is absolutely on me here, Softly.'

Softly shrugged, mouth shrunk to an impenitent asterisk.

'Can I have a go?' Bimbo said to the young man.

The young man carefully drew the katana back into the scabbard.

'I would say no.'

'For why? I just want a go.'

'I think you're mocking.'

'I am not mocking!' Bimbo said.

'I'd say he is mocking, lad,' Moira said.

'Bimbo, will you let the poor child alone,' Peader said with a gasp.

'The Alp boys think everything is a joke,' Moira said.

'Moira,' Bimbo said. 'You are an awful acute pain in the hole, do you know that.'

Moira cackled ruefully. 'And you're as easy as the breeze to rile.'

Rory slid from his seat and moved with surprising nimbleness up behind the young man. He enclosed his arms around the young man, squeezed and lifted. The young man ejected a startled yelp and began furiously paddling his long legs in the air, like a cartoon character. Bimbo grasped the sheathed katana and wrenched it free of the young man's grip. Rory then hefted the young man over to one of the lounge sofas, dropped him sideways on to the cushions and sat down on his shoulder, pinning him in place.

'Don't be wriggling,' Rory said as the young man thrashed and wheezed, his face turning bright pink.

'Ah, lads,' Mikey said.

Eustace went over and sat down on the young man's legs.

'Lads, come on,' Mikey said.

'Watch, now,' Bimbo said, delighted. He drew the katana from its scabbard. He held it up and out. The sword wobbled a bit. Bimbo tried to reproduce the fine arc the young man had cut in the air but swung loosely and at the apex of his swing the katana almost jumped free of his grasp.

Softly sprang up off his stool.

'Watch where you're flittering that thing,' he said.

'I am watching,' Bimbo said defensively, and slid the sword back into its scabbard.

The clubhouse door opened. Two men entered. The first man had his arm raised and was holding out a set of keys like they were a dead mouse.

'Some cretin left his keys in the middle of the car park

and they'd be still there only I trod on them getting out of the car,' he announced.

'It appears Derek is here,' said the second man to the first. 'It appears them two gentlemen over there are sitting on top of him.

'Of course they are,' said the man with the keys.

It was clear the two men were related to the young man with the sword. They had the same gangling cuts to their bearing and the same shining, disconnected look in their eyes. The second man was holding a golf club, a driver with a big, solid head.

Denise walked up to the first man.

'Give here,' she said. 'They belong to us.'

The man drew the keys close to his chest, considered them.

'These are the keys to a Mondeo,' he said. 'What sort of reckless idiot is dropping the keys to a Mondeo out in an empty car park? Believe me, I'll take the Mondeo off your hands if you're that fed up with it.'

'The keys were pegged out there,' Denise said. 'I am here with a big giant manbaby and it was the manbaby went and pegged the keys out the door about five minutes ago in a fit of temper.'

'Do not call me a manbaby,' Softly said.

'You mean to say that lad purposefully pegged the keys to a Mondeo out into the car park?' said the first man.

'Thank you for picking them up,' Denise said, her hand out.

'Well I honestly don't know if the kind of person who would do a thing like that merits having their keys returned to them,' the first man said.

'I would entirely agree,' Denise said, 'only *I* need them keys to get home. The manbaby can walk, for all I care.'

'I SAID THAT'S OUR LITTLE BROTHER YOU'VE YOUR HOLES PARKED ON,' the man with the club roared in the direction of Rory and Eustace.

The young man – Derek – had more or less stopped thrashing and was lying limply beneath the brothers' substantial behinds.

'To be fair, there's a very good reason for this arrangement,' Eustace said.

'Your little brother strode in out of the wilds with a sword on his person,' Rory said.

'A katana,' Eustace said.

'A replica of a katana,' Bimbo said.

'A replica of a katana,' Rory said. 'In any case, what kind of a person does that? A person in needs of subduing, I'd say.'

'That fella needs more than subduing is what that fella needs,' said the first man.

'Come up,' said the second man. He strode forward, brandishing the golf club two-handedly and with evident purpose. Rory and Eustace, intuiting the man's capability, got on to their feet and stepped clear of Derek. Derek tried to scramble upright. The man drew the golf club back over his shoulder and swung down with all his might, the head of the club landing on the forearm Derek instinctively raised. There was a crack and Derek screamed. The man with the club got off three decisive swings, connecting meatily with Derek's limbs and torso as he flailed backwards off the sofa and tried to cram his entire body in under the tabletop.

The man with the club ceased his attack. He paced around in a little circle, breathing heavily through his nose.

'Come out from under that table, Derek,' he said with no venom in his voice, just an even brotherly solicitude.

'What's all this in aid of?' Rory said.

'Who are you?' said the first man.

'Who are you?' Rory said back.

'We're Derek's brothers,' said the man with the club.

'And what did your brother do warrants getting absolutely laced out of it with a golf club?' Eustace asked.

'He topped Mammy's Sphynx,' the first man said.

'Hah?' Eustace said.

'The mammy's Sphynx,' said the man with the club. 'It's a breed of cat. High pedigree, very delicate, very expensive. We got it for the mammy last year when the oul fella finally kicked the bucket.'

'Be way of company for her,' the first man said.

'The oul fella was useless company, but he was company all the same,' the man with the club said.

'Daddy was an awful prick is what Daddy was,' Derek said from under the table.

'Shut up, Derek,' the first man said.

'Eleven hundred euro,' the man with the club said.

'Eleven hundred euro of an outlay for that creature and it hadn't a hair on its entire body,' the first man said. 'The heating bills she was landed with.'

'The mammy had to keep the house equatorial the whole year round, the rads on full pelt,' the man with the golf club said.

'And the awful expensive food it could only eat.'

'And all the shots it had to keep getting.'

'It was an awful oul sickly oul wrinkly oul bald oul yoke.'

'It looked like a shaved ballbag with four legs stuck on it is what it looked like,' the man with the club said.

'But she loved it,' the first man said.

'She loved it and this useless article under the table here only had to go after it with a sword,' the man with the club said. 'Managed to stab the poor thing to death and near killed the mother too with the fright he put on her.'

'What sort of a man has it in him to top a cat?' the first man said.

Derek was silent under the table, his long feet sticking out.

'That cat was always mocking me,' he said eventually.

The man with the club sighed. 'It was a cat, Derek.'

'They are not the most amenable creatures, but still,' the first man said.

'Come out now until we go home, Derek,' the man with the club said.

'No,' the young man said.

'Derek, come out before I drag you out and make a further mock of you in front of all your new friends.'

'No. You've my head ringing.'

The man with the club darted forward and got a hold of one of Derek's heels. Derek wrapped his arms around the centre beam of the table. The man with the club began towing Derek. The table toppled over but Derek clung steadfastly to it and dragged it thunking along with him across the burgundy carpet.

'Ah, here,' Bimbo said, stepping across the path of the man with the club, fist tight around the handle of the katana. 'I'm not saying he didn't do what you said he did, but touched as he is I can't let you be dragging that fella out the door like that. It's not right.'

The man with the club stopped and looked at Bimbo. Derek looked up from the floor at Bimbo.

'That's your own brother you're making a spectacle of,' Rory said to the man with the club.

'I know Derek seems ... soft,' the first man said. 'But the truth is he is a living trial.'

'Sure aren't we all?' Bimbo said. 'Aren't we all living trials to one another.'

'Maybe it's you two should leave and let that fella with us,' Eustace said.

Rory and Eustace had arranged themselves so that they were now flanking Bimbo.

The man with the club considered the dense wall of the Alps boys. Muscle-wise, what was there was flabby, and without definition, but there must have been a good seven hundred pounds of it combined. He looked at the first man. The first man shrugged. The man with the club dropped Derek's foot to the floor.

'Ow,' said Derek.

'He should be in a home is where he should be,' the man with the club said. 'But the mother wouldn't have it. Well she has gone and learned her lesson now.'

The two men began to back towards the clubhouse door.

'Here,' Denise McIlenden shouted at the first man. 'The keys.'

The first man checked, looked at the keys in his hand, lobbed them at Denise.

'Were you really going to try and set on me with a replica sword?' the man with the club asked Bimbo.

'I can't be sanctioning you boys coming in here leather-
ing the shite out of this young fella and dragging him
around the place like a bit of lawn furniture, no matter
what he done,' Bimbo said.

The man with the club sighed.

'Setting on your own brother,' he said. 'I know it's not
right. I know there's nothing in it that's a credit to me. But
what that fella sees fit to put her through.'

'We don't deserve them, do we?' Bimbo said. 'Our
mothers.'

'We don't,' said the man with the club. He tucked the
driver under his arm, took out his wallet, flicked through it.

'Here,' he said to the first man, 'have you a twenty?'

'What?' said the first man.

'Have you a twenty? Give it here.'

The first man made a face, but complied. The man with
the club took the twenty, added a twenty of his own and
handed the money over to Mikey.

'The next round,' the man with the club said. 'Derek,
I'm sorry I took Daddy's club to you.'

'I'm sore all over,' Derek said.

'I'm afraid that can't be helped now.'

The two men left.

'Well, now,' Bimbo said.

'Wasn't that very good of them,' Moira said, nodding at
the money in Mikey's hand.

'Come up here, young fella,' Rory said, extending a
hand to the young man still on his back on the floor. Derek
accepted and Rory hauled him up on to his feet.

'You look as shook,' Moira said to Derek.

'Mikey, will you run this man a big glass of water,' Rory said. 'When you're shook you need to hydrate.'

'If you are peckish, I've a heap more toasties in the fridge,' Mikey said.

'I have no appetite on me,' Derek said.

'Well done, the Alps boys,' Peader Ginty said.

'Aye, well done on not getting your heads cracked open, much as you were trying,' Softly said.

'Softly,' Denise said, 'shut up.'

'What?' Softly said.

'The Alps boys put themselves on the line for that odd-ball of a young fella,' Denise said. 'He was getting a beating and they saved him from much worse. And what did you do? Pegged the keys to your Mondeo into the night like a child. That goon was right about you.'

'I didn't heed a thing that goon was saying about me.'

'More's the pity. Well done, the Alps boys,' Denise said and stepped over to Bimbo. He cleared his throat and was about to correct his posture but she was already in on top of him. He could smell the lime and gin off her. She kissed him on the cheek and he felt her arms slide from his shoulders like scarves of silk and Denise McIlenden was away from him, moving towards the door.

'Where are you off to?' Softly said.

Denise opened the door. 'You know what I've noticed about you, Softly.'

Softly said nothing.

'You're as stingy,' Denise continued. 'You've the stingi-est outlook on the world. You're incapable of extending even the tiniest untainted compliment to anyone, about anything, and it is awful wearying to be around.'

She left.

All within listened to the whinny and growl of the Mondeo's engine out in the car park, watched the headlights bloom on the clubhouse windows and the crackle of the gravel as the car turned and left.

'Well, now,' Moira said.

Mikey placed a pint of tap water on the counter.

'Drink,' Bimbo said, guiding Derek back on to the stool. The young man gulleted down the water in one go, exhaled and wiped his mouth.

'Good lad. This is yours,' Bimbo said and handed the replica katana back.

'Face is shining up decently, now,' Rory said.

'He landed a rap on your head, did he?' Eustace asked.

'He got me everywhere,' Derek said.

'Where's it hurt most?' Bimbo asked.

'All over.'

'Can you move your arm freely?' Bimbo said. He took hold of the young man's forearm and moved it in a slow circle. 'How sore is that?'

'It's . . . not too bad.'

'Did you really stab your mother's cat?' Eustace said.

'I'm not proud of that.'

'Well, you wouldn't be,' Eustace said.

'No,' Derek said. He licked his lips and fainted forward.

'Watch,' Bimbo said.

All the colour had evaporated from Derek's complexion. He dropped his head and with a lurch of his shoulders all the water came back up in an opaque gout, drenching his shins and shoes and the carpet.

'Ah, now,' Bimbo said, the toes of his workboots spattered.

'I don't feel good,' Derek moaned into his chest, and fell forward again, Bimbo catching him so he did not land on the floor.

Bimbo ducked down to see Derek's face. His eyes were rolling in his head.

'I think he's out.'

'Put him on his back on the ground,' Moira said.

'I am ringing Castlebar General,' Mikey said.

'He could swallow his tongue. Don't let him swallow his tongue,' Moira said, up off her stool. Peader began also to rise.

'Daddy, don't put yourself out,' Moira said.

Bimbo tossed the sword to the floor and guided Derek's limp body down on to the carpet. He tapped the young man's cheek with two fingers.

'Does he have a pulse?' Rory asked.

'I don't know if I know how to do that,' Bimbo said, licking his thumb and sticking it right in under the young man's nose. He was sure he felt the slight cool dab of exhaled air.

'He is breathing, I reckon.'

'Hello—' said Mikey into his phone. He spluttered through a series of questions with the hospital operator, saying only that the young man had received a heavy accidental blow to the head. He relayed to the Alps the operator's instructions about keeping the head elevated and the airways unobstructed. 'OK,' said Mikey. 'OK, OK.'

'How long?' Rory said.

'Said the ambulance would be thirty minutes.'

'Thirty minutes!' Rory shouted. 'Here, get him up. Thirty minutes. We'll have him to Castlebar General in fucking half that.'

'That Hiace is a junkheap,' Moira said. 'No way you are doing the trip quicker than an ambulance.'

'She's lightning once she gets into her stride,' Rory said. 'Here, Softly, give us a hand.'

Softly hunkered down, grabbed Derek's spare leg. Bimbo had the other one, and Eustace and Rory each took a shoulder. The quartet lifted the young man up and began to stagger forward. Mikey came out from behind the bar and held the door. Moira picked the sword up off the floor then she and her father, towing his trolleybag, followed the men out into the night.

The four men crunched across the gravel, floundering one way and then the other, but they did not drop the young man's body, which sagged like a laden hammock between them. Bimbo glanced towards the floodlit pitch. There was now a cow under the crossbar, nibbling at the grass edging the rutted patches of the goalmouth.

Ahead of them, another cow was rubbing its ribs against a corner of the Hiace's grille. Bimbo saw and sensed more big shapes gliding around in the dark of the car park

'Cows,' Peader stated.

'Well spotted,' Bimbo said.

'Go on, get,' Rory said, and with his head butted the neck of the cow that was using the Hiace as a scratching post. It mooed and started away.

'Where'd they come out of, though?' Eustace said.

'The fencing is in an awful state down the far end of the grounds. They could be in from any of them fields adjacent,' Mikey said, reaching out to pat the haunch of a nearby ginger heifer.

'Never mind about the cows,' Bimbo demanded. He let down the young man's leg, pulled back the Hiace's side door, sprung in and commenced kicking a clearing amid the boxes of various-sized screws and the coiled yards of insulated wire. Rory, Eustace and Softly transferred the young man on to the van's dirt-caked mat.

Derek moaned, lifted his head up.

'What's happening?' he asked.

'We're saving your life is what's happening,' Bimbo said, the heel of his hand on Derek's chest to stay him from getting up.

'Am I dying?' Derek asked.

'No one is dying on our watch,' Bimbo declared.

Softly began clambering into the Hiace.

'What are you doing?' Bimbo asked.

'I want to help,' Softly said.

'Go on, so,' Bimbo said, and moved his haunches so Softly could enter.

Rory got in behind the wheel and Eustace joined him up front.

'Are you OK to drive with pints on you?' asked Mikey through the wound-down driver window.

Rory turned on the engine and considered the question.

'I would say I drive better with drink taken,' he said, 'because I know I have to be more careful.'

'Well, good luck,' Mikey said doubtfully, and rapped the side of the van.

There were dozens of cows stood around in the car park, gormless as wardrobes. Rory revved the engine, pounded the horn and inched the Hiace forward until the animals began to lumber out of the way. With a parting shout of 'Up Mayo' out the window and another beep, the Hiace snarled on to the main road and raced off into the night.

'Lord bless us and save us,' Moira said.

'Indeed,' Mikey said.

By the clubhouse entrance a wall light illuminated the backless wooden bench and pail of sand that denoted the smoking area. Peader wheeled his trolley over, and Moira and Mikey followed, Moira idly swishing the sword in the air.

Mikey sat down beside Peader and lit a cigarette, nodded at the sword. 'You forget to hand that over?'

'I suppose I did,' Moira said.

Mikey looked with dismay down the long dark length of the car park. He couldn't see the cows, but they were there.

'This place will be absolutely laced in shit tomorrow morning,' he said.

Moira was looking at the peeling band of Mikey's neck. She reached out and touched his skin, lightly, felt the seethe of the sunburn on the pads of her fingertips.

'That must hurt,' she said.

'Ah, it's grand,' Mikey said.

Moira propped the sword against the wall by the bench, opened her purse, brought out a small tube and squirted a curlicue of cream into her palm. She rubbed her palms together and stepped in behind Mikey.

'It's fine,' Mikey said.

'Don't be a boy.'

Moira's fingers were thin and hard, kneading in the cold of the cream. It did feel good. Mikey took a drag, relinquished a long sigh.

'I have to go in now and root out a flashlight and ascertain which field these cows got out of and then go ring whichever farmer they belong to.'

'Poor Mikey,' Moira said.

'Poor Mikey,' Peader agreed.

'You think that young fella will be all right?' Mikey asked.

'I would say the brother should have given him a few extra lashes while he was at it,' Moira said.

'Moira, stop,' Peader said.

'That fella was not right, Daddy. He had an awful sinister cut to him altogether.'

'He did admit to topping a cat,' Mikey said.

'No one's denying that's not usual behaviour,' Peader said.

'That buck was from another planet,' Moira said.

'Well, the Alps have him now,' Mikey said.

'Speaking of other planets,' Moira said.

'What have you got against the Alps anyway?' Mikey said. He held the cigarette up so Moira could take it over his shoulder.

Moira slapped her hands together, took the cigarette and stepped back from Mikey.

'*I drive better with drink taken,*' she scoffed. 'I guess you can't argue with that logic.'

'Sure won't you be driving home with a few on you yourself.'

'I will,' Moira said, 'but I won't be proud of it. That's the difference.'

'Are they proud of it?' Mikey asked.

Moira shrugged and took a drag.

'Oh, I'd love a go,' Peader said, watching his daughter smoke.

'You could have one puff,' Moira said, 'if it was just the one. But it wouldn't be, would it?'

'It would not,' Peader agreed. 'I think we will say good-night, young Mikey. I hope you get this mess sorted.'

Moira passed the cigarette back to Mikey.

'Keep the sword,' she told him.

'Goodnight,' Mikey said and watched the two walk off into the dark. Mikey was able to mark their progress by the wheedling rattle of Peader's trolley over the car park stones and the snorts of consternation that came from the invisible cows. Mikey smoked the remainder of the cigarette and studied the sky, the glimmering points of the stars, for the trace of a deliberate, fugitive movement, but none was forthcoming. He went into the clubhouse, rooted out a torch. Back at the smoking area, he hesitated by the sheathed sword, propped against the wall where Moira had left it. He picked it up and set off into the dark of the grounds, the light from his torch roving across the black in search of the rupture, or gap, or wherever it was the cows had come out of.

# WHOEVER IS THERE, COME ON THROUGH

EILEEN WATCHED the bus pull into the depot and the passengers debark, stiff and groggy, into the crisp November air, their breaths flashing like handkerchiefs in front of their faces. She was in her car, the window rolled all the way down, her arm slung out. She was smoking a cigarette but the cigarette had gone out and her arm had turned numb, not from the cold but from the pressure of its own hanging weight. Eileen liked the sensation, as if her arm were holding its breath.

The crowd dispersed, leaving one man lurking under the eave of the shelter. He had a Slazenger sports bag bunched against his ribs, long wrists dangling from his coat cuffs, and a pink, animate nose, twitching like a dog's. It was Murt's gait and it was Murt's head. Eileen had known Murt since they were both thirteen – a dozen years now – and his frame had never lost the stringy, unfinished quality of adolescence, though he had since acquired a little belly.

Eileen dropped the dead smoke and hauled her sleeping

arm inside the car and on to her lap. She jabbed her other
thumb into the crease of her palm. The flesh was cool,
waxen, but already she could feel it coming on, the reviving
fizz of the nerves. When the bristling subsided, she opened
the door and got out, raised her refreshed arm into the air.
Murt gathered the folds of his coat collar and set off from
under the eaves.

When he was near enough, she said, 'Welcome back to
planet Earth.'

'They still calling it that?' he said.

'They are.'

'I told you, you didn't have to come.'

'I know,' Eileen said.

He went to hug her, and she stepped away from the
door to let him.

He asked her to go to his Uncle Nugent's. He did not say
if his uncle was expecting him, or what his mother would
have to say about that. Murt did not make any mention
of the mother. Eileen had resolved not to ask too many
questions. As far as she knew, on this occasion Murt had
entered the hospital voluntarily and the hospital had now
consented to his discharge; Eileen took this to mean that
he was over the worst of it, had managed to once again
step back from the ledge of himself. It would be up to him
to talk about it or not. So Eileen concentrated on getting
him across town, subdued on a weekday afternoon, the
slivers of ice pulverised into the pores of the macadam giving the road a sullen shine.

They idled on a red at a T-junction.

'Who won the US election?' Murt asked.

She told him.

'Whoa,' he said flatly.

The election had been two weeks earlier. Eileen figured Murt already knew who'd won; the question was a way of letting her know how out of it he was – at least back then.

'We could go to McDonald's,' Eileen said.

'What even are they called?' Murt said. Eileen glanced over at him. He had his shoulders ducked forward and was looking through the windshield at a building that used to be a bank, then something else, but was now a bank again.

'What are what even called?'

'I want to say cornices,' he said. 'Turrets, maybe. Those sculpted bits of stone, those patterned bits, at the very top. I don't have a clue, but.'

Eileen looked up. The stone along the roof of the building had a row of vertical recesses carved into it, the recesses filled with scraps of blond, stale-looking snow.

'What you don't know,' Murt said. 'It's only when you stop to take stock you realise. I can, for instance, be reading a book.'

'And you look up,' Eileen said.

'Exactly,' he said. 'Like, what was I just reading? I can spend thirty minutes devoutly banging through a book, rereading sentences just to savour them. And a minute later I'm consulting the wall and I can't recall a blessed.'

'I get that, completely,' Eileen said.

'I mean, my concentration is absolutely *totalled* most of the time anyway, just gone. But now and then I'll lull myself into thinking, yeah, yeah, the head's getting sharp again—Oh, go,' he said, meaning the light.

Eileen looked. Green.

Murt's bag was squeezed in front of his shins in the footwell. He mumbled at her that his phone was dead. Eileen said there was a portable charger in the glovebox. 'Resurrecting the profiles,' he said, thumbing at the screen.

At McDonald's, Murt ordered two Happy Meals for himself, a chocolate milkshake and a coffee. They took a booth.

'Always enjoy the tension,' he said. 'Waiting to see if they'll ask if there's actually a child with you.'

Eileen thought Murt's mentioning a child might prompt him to ask after her son, Ashleigh.

'I'm thinking they're obliged to give you whatever you want in any case,' she said.

'Yeah, but there are the rules and there's the spirit of the thing,' Murt said, turning the nubbin of a chicken nugget between his fingers. 'Strikes me I've been pining for a taste of exactly this. And you knew.'

'I wanted to come anyway,' Eileen said.

'Look,' he said. There were two lads at the counter. One was in a Chicago Bulls bomber jacket, the other had a frayed cast on his wrist and a round, ugly, floridly freckled face, their heads cocked back with their mouths open, contemplating the overhead screens of the menu.

'The Heads,' Murt said. 'The Heads, the Heads, the Heads.'

Lunchtimes back in secondary school, he and Eileen would walk around the town pegging cold chips at pigeons and inventing classifications for passers-by. The Heads was what they used to call a certain type of local, the ones to whom it would never occur to leave. Eileen, it seemed, had become one of them after all.

On the way to his uncle's, Murt said that he was tired. Tired was a vague descriptor, and anything vague was treacherous, but Eileen didn't want to push. Nugent's house was a bungalow with a pebble-dash job so pock-marked it looked as if the facade had taken heavy artillery fire. There were two cars in the drive. Murt did not invite her in. He said, 'Thank you for the lift, Eileen.'

'Take her handy and I'll give you a buzz soon,' she said.

Eileen replayed their interaction on the drive home. She had to be careful. There was the danger, after one of his bad periods, of reading meaning into Murt's every blink and syllable. She had arranged to work only evenings this week behind Naughton's bar, so that she could get over to Murt in the mornings or early afternoons, which would at least oblige him to be up at a reasonable hour. Not that she wanted to impose structure on him. But she wanted to be there if structure was what he needed.

They'd met when the girls Eileen hung out with fell in with the boys Murt hung out with. Murt was the morose but funny one of the group, and played the hypochondriac, anxious, would-be depressive so well and so pitilessly that Eileen was surprised to find out that he actually was all of those things. When they were sixteen, he confessed to a crush on her. She told him that she wanted to stay friends. A few weeks later, he went into the hospital for the first time. Eileen blamed herself, until he eventually wrote a gruellingly detailed email assuring her that she had noth-ing to do with it, or not more than anything else. She would not have believed him without that qualification. This latest stint was Murt's fourth hospitalisation. He'd tried to tell her once what it was like. He said it was as if everything were always turning endlessly over, turning into something else, inside him, and Eileen's understanding was that it simply never stopped.

The next time Eileen arrived at Nugent's, there were again two cars in the drive. A pug dog was padding around the lawn. Its jowled puss and weepy eyes tracked Eileen as she got out of her car. It kept watching as she walked around the bonnet to retrieve a carton of doughnuts from the passenger side. The dog belonged to Sara Duane, Jamie's *beoir*, which meant that Jamie, Murt's big brother, must be there too. The front door was closed but not locked, a gesture of etiquette still resolutely practised among certain of the older generation and which meant: whoever is there, come on through. As Eileen went down the hall, she could hear the scattering cold points of a young man's laughter, Jamie's laughter.

Eileen tapped on the kitchen door, pushed it open. Nugent was sitting on a ragged little settee with a trucker cap covering his bald spot. Murt was at the kitchen table in a cement-coloured hoodie, his laptop in front of him. Jamie was up and in motion, wearing an olive-green forestry jacket over a T-shirt, sweatpants, and a pair of battered Chelsea boots, the heels of the boots snapping like fingers as he paced the planked floor. Sara Duane was in an easy chair, drinking Calpol cough medicine straight out of the bottle, a purple tinge banding her top lip.

'Currency is anyway a legacy structure,' Jamie said.

'Sorry for interrupting,' Eileen said, looking from Nugent

to Jamie and then Murt. Murt had the glassy, heaped dis-
position of one routed recently from his bed.

'Eileen,' Nugent said. He rose to his feet, looked down
at the settee, and sighed. 'Change,' he said, 'is the bane of
my existence,' and bent to recover the coins that had just
seeped from his pockets.

Nugent, a man once unthinkingly robust, had suffered
a stroke several years back. Among the litany of mutinies
perpetrated by his body on his body was a lasting deform-
ity to his hands: each thumb and forefinger had wrenched
back and locked in place, an effect that surgery had only
partially reversed. His thumbs remained severely kinked,
like claws, obliging Nugent to roughly sweep at the cush-
ion with one palm and catch the splattering coins in the
other.

'Coins are at least aesthetically pleasing objects. Notes
are just dirty paper,' Jamie said.

'We're on economics now,' Nugent said to Eileen. 'You
already missed a lecture on biology.'

'Currency's a sentiment we can let go of at any time,'
Jamie said. 'We just don't want to yet, but rest assured.'

'Not going to happen,' Murt said.

'Trust me,' Jamie replied. 'Currency, computers, they
are just technologies, and it's in the nature of technologies
to go away. A thing arrives, it proliferates, it grows into
ubiquity. And, like everything else that reaches ubiquity, it
one day disappears.'

'Your dog is outside, so you know,' Eileen said.

'I do know,' Sara said.

'Cheerio has a ferocious tolerance for his own company,'
Jamie said. 'Which is commendably undogly of him.'

'I would say he looks a little bit lost out there,' Eileen said.

'He came out of his mammy's crease looking exactly as lost,' Jamie said. 'Don't judge a thing off him by that look.'

'What are you saying about my dog?' Sara said to Jamie. 'And she's a she, for Christ's sakes. Millionth time I'm telling you.' She had the pinched, flushed look of someone enduring something viral.

'I brought doughnuts,' Eileen said.

'Doughnuts,' Jamie sneered.

'Doughnuts,' Sara repeated.

'What's wrong with doughnuts?' Eileen said.

'Nothing. Only there's no credible way for a Mayo accent to say *dough-nutz*,' Jamie said.

It was Eileen's opinion that if you wanted demented, if you wanted pathology, here was Jamie: with his vicious jabber and his incoherent clothes, his brain like a door with a busted latch, incapable of ever being shut. The forestry jacket was pure Jamie. Out of technical college he'd managed to get a job in which he was paid very well to sit in a Portakabin in the Belleek Woods and read the paper while polite middle-class ramblers visiting from Dublin and the odd school tour trekked around the trails and the ruins. Last year he'd been suspended and then fired after it was discovered he was taking payments to let travellers burn rubbish on a site in the woods. The smoke had almost completely killed off a listed species of weed that grew wild there. Jamie maintained that the real reason he was let go was that he'd consorted with travellers, treating them with what he insisted was dignity while the council racked their brains to find a way to run them out of town altogether. Eileen recalled the second car outside. She wondered if Jamie had also managed to shack up with Nugent. Jamie had been the standard superior big brother, oscillating between picking on and protecting Murt, and still possessed an occult hold over him without even trying. Eileen could already hear Jamie's influence in Murt's voice.

'Another problem being, economics is a theology now,' Murt said.

'Absolutely,' Jamie said. 'Absolutely. And the worst one there is.'

'Is he here too, so?' Eileen asked Nugent, nodding at Jamie.

'In what sense?' Nugent asked.

'In the sense is he staying here too.'

'For a spell,' Jamie said. 'Would be the situation.'

'Define spell,' Nugent said to Jamie, a little irritated. Then, to Eileen, 'I made the mistake of not offering terms and little has been forthcoming.'

'Nuge understands solidarity,' Jamie said. 'And is a tender-hearted cunt underneath it all.'

'Nuge is frankly sound,' Murt said.

'We love him,' Jamie said.

'Stop,' Nugent said.

Eileen came over to the table and popped open the doughnut carton. She'd bought five, figuring one apiece for Murt, Nugent and herself, with an extra one each for the boys. 'Have at them,' she said.

'These from the Maxol out at the Tesco?' Jamie asked.

'Yeah,' Eileen said.

'Excellent. They are of course not good, but they are

the best you will get in this corner of the world,' Jamie
said, lifting a glazed ring and taking a bite.

'I want like a half,' Sara said. Jamie tore his doughnut in
half and tossed her the bitten part.

'Prickhole,' she said, and threw it back at him. It landed
on the floor.

Nugent said he would put on the tea.

'I was thinking we could go into town, maybe,' Eileen
said to Murt. 'Or a walk.'

'Thanks, Eileen,' Murt said, rising from his seat to reach
for a doughnut. Jamie leaned in and measuredly thwacked
the carton down the table towards his little brother.

'And how's Big Devaney?' Jamie asked Eileen, meaning
her partner, Mark.

'He's sound.'

'And how's your little buck? What's your little buck
called again?'

'Ashleigh.'

'Ashleigh,' Jamie repeated. 'Only I saw Devaney's other
boy, the teenage lad, in town the other day.'

'That would be Danny.'

'It's an uncanny business,' Jamie said.

'What is?' Murt asked.

'Children,' Jamie said.


Eileen and Murt were walking the path by the river in the
Belleek Woods. It was only gone two in the afternoon, but
the sky was already so grey it was like being on the moon, the
light a kind of exhausted residue. To their right coursed
the Moy, dark as stout and in murderous spate; to their left
high conifers stood like rows of coats on coat racks. Eileen

was smoking, a sheltering hand cupped over her mouth, miz-
zle prickling her face; Murt was in a woollen hat and gloves
borrowed from his uncle. They'd agreed to walk the length
of the woods and were both so soaked it would have taken
more resolve to abandon the walk than to keep going.

'Nuge is an incel,' Murt said.

'Incel?'

'Involuntary celibate.'

'What's that when it's at home?'

'What it sounds like.'

'And in what sense is Nuge one of them cells?' Eileen said.

'Incel,' Murt said. 'And he is one in the sense he's never
known how to get any – and never will. That's the problem with sex. In order to know how to get any, you need to
have already managed to figure out how to get some. And
Nuge is too innocent.'

'Innocent,' Eileen said.

'In his heart, Nuge is an innocent. A man without guile.'

Murt and Jamie's father had been a generally useless
article who drank, and left the family to move to England
when Murt was ten, ostensibly for work. They'd stopped
hearing from him years ago. Nugent, his younger brother,
had always been one of those men who spent a lot of time
with children, back when that wasn't looked at sceptically.
He'd stewarded football games, volunteered in the com-
munity centre, and let Murt or Jamie stay at his place
whenever they got too much for their mother.

'He was always that way,' Murt went on, 'even before
the stroke. Small towns are incubators for these men. It's
not even that they are secretly gay or anything like that.
They just never developed the cop to have anything to do

with it at all. These are the men who faithfully do the messages, by foot, every day for the mother, year in and year out, until one of them drops dead.'

A few days with Jamie had entirely contaminated Murt's style of speaking, though he was energised, which was good.

'Is Nugent's mother alive?' Eileen asked.

'She's not, but that doesn't matter. It goes towards my point.'

'And how is *your* mother?'

'That's not the question.'

'I was only asking.' Murt did not respond. He was looking straight ahead. Jogging at them through the hanging vapour was a man in a sopping T-shirt. The number 2012 was emblazoned on it in large white print and for a moment Eileen felt disoriented, as if that sequence of digits, the year they represented, were an unreachably long way away into the future, instead of already gone. Eileen and Murt parted and the man passed between them, eyes resentfully intent upon the middle distance.

'Cullen. Keith Cullen, that was,' Eileen said.

'Loon, in this weather,' Murt said.

'You're telling me.'

'In the locker room at school once he thumped me on the side of the head for I forget what,' Murt said.

'I could imagine, though,' Eileen said. 'Something maybe about his sister probably, or his *beoir*, some no doubt enlightened remark right out of my mouth.'

After a while, Eileen said, 'I think Nugent's all right.'

'I'm not saying he's not all right.'

They kept walking. Murt felt around in his jacket pocket and pulled out a packet of hard toffees. He grubbed a sweet from its cellophane wrapper and lodged it inside his jaw, offered Eileen one. She took a last drag of her cigarette and flicked it into the Moy.

'Let me tell you,' Murt said, sighing.

'Tell me,' Eileen said.

'Being depressed is like being in a dream. The suspicion is that everyone you meet is actually depressed too, only they don't know it. Or worse. The suspicion is that they're just aspects of you, manifestations.'

'I don't follow,' Eileen admitted.

'Cullen, for instance,' Murt went on. 'I was just thinking about school this morning. I was thinking about how awful I was back then, and how I was just this wretched little streak of jism. And I was thinking about how many deserved lumps I got, and how Cullen was just one of the many lads who imparted them lumps to me. And then there he is. What is he, then, if not a manifestation?'

'I did want to ask how your mother is, Murt.'

'Jesus. Eileen. Fuck. How about: how is Eunice?'

'Eunice is fine,' Eileen said tonelessly.

'Eunice is paying penance for other people's sins, is what poor Eunice is doing,' Murt said, agitated.

'She is,' Eileen said.

Murt broke into a waddling jog. He went off into the rain, and like a boxer he drew his fists up in front of his face, swinging one out and then the other, imparting lumps to heads that were not there.

They were in Eileen's car in the drive of her house. Murt had his head at an angle, cuffing himself under his ear, runnels of rain striping his cheek.

'I will towel the head and then.'

'Sure,' Eileen said.

'No offence.'

'I know.'

Murt was always reluctant to come in. It didn't matter who was around. They went through to the kitchen. Ashleigh was seated at the kitchen table with his half-brother, Danny, in their different-coloured school uniforms, Ashleigh's a maroon jumper over a grey shirt, Danny's a pastel-blue shirt and navy tie. Ashleigh was six, Danny fourteen. Danny had a pistachio between his teeth. Ashleigh was watching him.

'What's this?' Eileen said.

Danny bit down on the pistachio with just enough pressure to split the shell. There was a pair of bowls in front of him. He dropped the kernel into one bowl and deposited the fragments of the husk into the other. This performance, Eileen figured, was for Ashleigh's benefit. It was a habit of Ashleigh's to set challenges for Danny, like popping the tab on a Coke can without letting the foam spurt, or completing the level of a video game. These challenges were always safely rudimentary, Ashleigh anxious only to see Danny demonstrate his worldly capability, and Danny always obliged.

'Anyone here going to actually eat any pistachios?' Eileen asked.

'I'm demonstrating a technique,' Danny said.

'I see that.'

'Da likes them,' Ashleigh said.

'Da likes to do that himself. They'll go stale out like that,' Eileen said.

'That's that, so,' Danny said to Ashleigh, flashing the younger boy a regretful glance as he ran his fingers along the resealable top of the packet. Danny looked at Eileen and then looked away. Danny was as contained and as opaque as any teenage boy, she supposed. He generally spoke to Eileen only when prompted, but did so in a considered and even manner in which she could never decode any sarcasm or hostility. Danny would have been within his rights to hate Eileen. Danny's mother was Eunice. Eunice had been Mark's first wife, was actually, still, his only wife, because they were separated but not divorced. Eileen was the reason Mark had left Eunice. There had been drama, not least because Eileen had been only nineteen, and Mark Devaney almost twice that, when she'd fallen pregnant with Ashleigh, but in the end Eunice, the wronged woman, had been the one to leave town. Danny had gone with her initially, but had returned a couple of years ago for secondary school.

Murt cleared his throat and eased back out into the hall. 'Will do the hair,' he said, and went upstairs.

Ashleigh sucked in his cheeks, jabbed out his tongue, and crossed his eyes.

'Stop,' Eileen said.

'How's Murt?' Danny said.

'He's good.'

'Good,' Danny said, fiddling now with the zipper of his football kitbag, on the seat beside him. Danny played the trumpet, and kept the instrument wrapped in a bit of newspaper in the bag. He played in the school band, played, albeit under some duress, at the parties his father was partial to throwing in the house, and he was good enough to pick and choose gigs with several local outfits. It mildly appalled Eileen that the boy carted this beautiful brass instrument around with his balled-up socks and stinking boots, but she figured that was the point. The kitbag was a gesture of deliberate negligence on Danny's part, a protest not against his ability but against his obligation to that ability.

'Any gigs coming up?' Eileen asked him.

'Them lads in the funk band are after me to play out in Enniscrone next Thursday.'

'School night.'

'I know. It pays, though.'

'They're the ones. What are they called again, them lads?'

'They go by White Chocolate.' Danny smirked.

'Say it to Mark.'

'I didn't say I was going. I said I was asked.'

'Well, say it to Mark.'

'And Da's birthday's in January. Reckon he'll enlist me in some capacity.'

'How old is Da now?' Ashleigh asked.

'How old do you think?' Eileen said.

'Em. Em. Seventy,' Ashleigh said.

'I'm going to tell him you said that,' Eileen said. She looked down at the bowls in front of Danny. 'Will you at least eat some of them?'

Danny frowned and placed a nut into his mouth. Eileen's phone vibrated. It was a text from Murt.

*sorry have headed off*

Eileen looked at the phone, then at the boys. She went upstairs to the bathroom. The window was up off the sash, the cold coming in. She looked around the empty, small space, drew back the crackly sheath of the shower curtain even though she knew there was nothing behind it. She closed the window.

'Murt,' she whispered, like he was just out of sight. 'Murt. Murt.'

She rang Murt and it went to voicemail. She texted.

*did u just go out the window??*

She went back downstairs, out into the drive. Her car was empty. There was no one out on the street. The phone beeped.

*yeah*

*why??*

*took a notion just had to go sorry hun*

Eileen went back inside and rang Murt, but it went to voicemail again. After a few minutes, Murt sent a flurry of texts.

*am grand laughing at this now*

*just wanted to see if i cld get down off shed roof into garden*

*& i did it was fun*

*jogging home feels good stitch in side tho*

*be sorry if i fell & done an angle*

*ankle! Good day had fun*

Eileen did not reply straight away. She texted when she was on her way to Naughton's.

*hun id say your not right in the head but u know that!! into work now x*


Over the next couple of weeks Eileen took Murt for drives. They went to Enniscrone beach and stood on a dune crest and watched the Atlantic gather in long, wobbling furrows and smack on to the shore. Eileen took Murt to the dole to sign on, took him to the cineplex to watch the feature they mutually adjudged the dumbest-looking, took him to the pharmacist for his refills, into town for new shoes. Christmas came and went. Eileen gave Murt a Jack & Jones shirt of grey denim.

One day Murt rang her for a change, and Eileen's body braced as if she were a passenger in a swerving car.

'Jesus Christ,' Murt said.

'Yeah?' Eileen croaked.

'Jamie's got that Duane one pregnant.'

'Oh, Lord,' Eileen said.

'Nuge is taking us out tonight for drinks. I thought maybe.'

'I'll see,' Eileen said.

'If you wanted,' Murt said.

'No, I'll see,' Eileen said. 'I just might need to switch a shift around.'

When Eileen walked into Kennedy's she found Nugent, Murt, Jamie and Sara at the very back of the lounge. Breedge, Murt and Jamie's mother, was there too. She was a white-haired and thin woman, seated securely between her sons, the way a mother has every right to be.

'Congratulations,' Eileen blurted, at everyone.

Sara stood up, took in a big breath, exhaled. 'This is mad,' she said, and hugged Eileen, something like delirium in the whites of her eyes. Jamie absently lifted a leg to let Sara sit back down beside him. Eileen looked at Murt, handsome in the shirt she'd got him, a hand on the little mound of his paunch as if he were the one who was pregnant. At the very end of the table Nugent was already rising.

'Sit down, Eileen, and I will get you a drink.'

'Sure I'll get one myself.'

'You will not,' Nugent said. 'What do you drink?' He looked at Murt. 'What does she drink?'

'Stop, a gin and tonic so,' Eileen said.

'Good girl.'

'Hello, Eileen,' Breedge said.

'Hello.'

'Can you believe this?'

'I can't!'

'This is some arrangement. What was it you used to always say, Jamie, about having kids?' Breedge said, looking sidelong at her son.

'I used to always say you should need a licence,' Jamie said.

'And now look,' Breedge said. 'See how it happens. It just happens, Jamie.'

'I stand by the principle,' Jamie said.

'Well, it's happened now, and that's that,' Breedge said. She had long fingers with smashed-looking knuckles. The way her hands wreathed her drink made Eileen think of the roots of trees that crack out of and then fuse with the pavement.

'It all's going on,' Breedge said. 'It just keeps barrelling ahead.'

'I'm guessing this would be life you're talking about, Mother,' Jamie said.

'You. A daddy. I don't know,' Breedge said. 'What do you think, Eileen?'

'Well, you can't prepare. Not really, I don't think. But they are going to be fine,' she said, looking at Jamie and Sara.

'Of course they'll be fine,' Breedge said.

'We won't be fine,' Jamie said. 'We'll be absolutely fucked.'

'Shut up,' Sara said, nudging him in the ribs.

'Boys do tend to melancholy,' Breedge said. 'Let him get it out of his system now and he might be in a right shape for when that baby arrives.'

Murt cleared his throat. 'Well done, but,' he said to Jamie, and raised his drink.

'The best day of your life,' Breedge said, 'is the day you realise it's no longer your own.'

Eileen drank too much because everyone drank too much. It was Nugent's fault; Nugent was being stealthily and lethally generous, nipping to the bar to conjure rounds between rounds, pre-empting other people as their turn to buy approached. When he wasn't buying drinks, he was sitting at his spot at the far end of the horseshoe-shaped booth, his rigid hands curled either side of his drink, sipping with a straw at his Jameson-and-ice and looking so pleased with himself he seemed almost tearful. Eileen went to the toilet and came back to the bar determined to order a round, her drunkenness like a patiently smouldering fire in the back of her head that she did not, as yet, have to address putting out. Jamie was there, heavy-lidded, breathing through his nose like a stabled horse.

'Your mother is in some way with the news,' Eileen said.

'She's processing,' Jamie said.

'You are going to be fine.'

'Are you fine?'

'What?'

'Never mind me. Are you fine, Eileen?'

'I am.'

'I know you are,' Jamie said, his mouth gone beady, unrepentant with drink. 'You are armour-plated.'

'I'm what?' Eileen said.

'You are a tank, Eileen. You just smash over things and you keep going.'

'What's that mean?'

'Murt. That boy is struggling, in case you didn't know.'

'I do know.'

'If I were in your shoes I know what I'd be saying. I'd be saying that I am trying to help. But you have to take your boot off his throat. Just for a little while you have to take your boot off his throat.'

Eileen's body felt like a heavy coat she had neglected to remove, the blood in her face thick and clambering. She went to speak but her throat shied.

'Murt is my best friend. I care so much about Murt,' she was able to finally say in a thin, winded voice, as if she were trying to talk after a bout of sprinting.

'You care for him, Eileen,' Jamie said, 'but you have no pity for him. He is what he is. He is not like the rest of us. You have to accept that. You have to have a little pity.'

'I don't know what Murt wants. But I don't think he wants pity, not from me,' Eileen said.

Jamie turned himself around, placed an elbow on the bar. He looked towards their booth. The table was honey-combed with empties. Sara, Breedge, Murt and Nugent all looked wired and exhausted.

'Murt will be moving back in with the mother shortly, did he tell you?'

'No,' Eileen said.

'That's why she's come out, really. Babby aside. It's difficult, but they are friends again.'

'I think that's good, anyway,' Eileen said.

'Do you know why Murt went back into the hospital? Do you know why he came to stay with Nuge and us, which was, by the way, my idea?'

Eileen said nothing.

'Living with Murt? Give me a break. Just try it someday, Eileen. She rang me up the night he went back into the hospital and you know what she said to me? She said, "He had to go." She said, "It was me or it was him." Imagine having to say that about your own son.'

'Think what you like about me,' Eileen said.

'You tell me what's best for that boy,' Jamie said.

Eileen said nothing. Jamie took a drink of his drink.

'There is no best.'

The following week Murt moved back in with his mother and a fortnight after that Jamie and Sara got the go-ahead to move in with Sara's folks. The Duanes despised Jamie but for the sake of the baby they assented to having him under their roof. At Nugent's behest, Jamie left his car in his uncle's care. Nugent pleaded a convincing case: there was plenty of parking space and he would be happy to keep the tank topped up and take it for the occasional spin. Nugent's own car was an unsalvageable relic, the tyres flat, gummed to the ground. It was Jamie's car Nugent used. He tried a week after Jamie and Sara left, on a Sunday evening, guiding the car into the cobweb-raftered garage at the back of his house and running a length of amputated garden hose from the exhaust pipe in through the driver's window. He drank heavily beforehand and swallowed a dozen sleeping pills. Once he had the engine on, he tried to cover up the gap in the driver's window with masking tape, but peeling away the required length of tape proved too difficult, what mobility he still possessed baffled by the pills and the booze and the carbon monoxide swilling around his head: eventually he passed out, but he vomited the pills in his sleep and the garage was not an airtight enough structure to accommodate a sufficient build-up of gas. It was Murt who found him. He was dropping in a spare plate of roast dinner from his mother's and just said he knew, coming through the unlocked front door of the house, some charge to the untidy emptiness within: a clear bag of defrosted chicken thighs puddling in the sink, a cup with a cracked handle lying in a cold splat of tea on the floor, the door out to the back ajar.

'The garage door was down. Do you remember if the garage door is ever usually down? I don't know, but maybe that was it. Subliminally, maybe it was like I registered that. I went out and realised I could hear an engine. I got the door up and he was within, in the car. He looked inhuman. Face on him like week-old cat shit.'

Murt telling this to Eileen the Friday after he found Nugent, Nugent stabilised in the ICU in Galway, breathing on his own but still very frail, waking only briefly and not communicating when he did, the doctors as yet dicey on the prospective degree of brain damage, organ damage, everything. Eileen and Murt were in Staunton's, Eileen on Sprite, Murt on Guinness. Eileen had the day off. Murt had enrolled in an evening writing class held in the secondary school, and had a session later.

'Jamie's awful cut up about the car.'

'You would be,' Eileen said.

'I think he feels duped.'

'How's Sara?'

'She's good. They'd the first scan. The what-you-call. The sonogram. The womb. Might as well be footage of the moon.' Murt supped his Guinness. 'Jamie's insisting now he wants to sell the car. He says getting into it feels like climbing into someone's tomb.'

'Nugent's alive.'

'He gave it some try, though.'

'He won't get much for that yoke at this stage,' Eileen said. 'Scrappage, is my guess. Come up tonight, though. Mark's birthday. We're having people.'

'He says there's a cursed energy to the car now. A malignant charge, when he gets in,' Murt said.

'How's the writing class?'

'The class is fine. Sound skins. Everyone is seventy, but they bring in home-made scones every week.'

'Well, there you go,' Eileen said.


The party had been going for several hours by the time Murt showed. Eileen saw his head bobbing in the crowded sitting room. She picked up a bottle of Guinness and made her way towards him, stepping carefully over Ashleigh, sprawled with four other kids on the ground in front of the TV, refereeing who went next on the Xbox.

Murt saw her, put his head down, shouldered a channel towards her.

'Brought these with me if you don't mind,' Murt said. Two women and a man were following him. They were all old.

'Oh, God, of course not, love!'

'This is Freda, this is Margaret, and this is Tom,' Murt said. 'Everybody, this is Eileen.'

The women were smiling but looked a little apprehensive. Around them people heedlessly jostled and cawed.

'Come on and I'll get you a drink,' Eileen said gently.

'Go on, they're my crowd to babysit, I'll get them a drink,' Murt said.

Eileen let him go. Mark appeared beside her, slid his arm around her waist. 'Who on earth invited the biddies?'

'Murt brought them.'

'Murt. Well, fair play,' Mark said.

Some of Mark's friends produced a guitar and a squeeze-box. They played 'Sally MacLennane' and 'The Sick Bed of Cuchulainn', 'Johnny Jump Up' and 'Solsbury Hill' and 'Leave Me Alone'.

Mark found Danny hiding out in his bedroom, and cajoled him downstairs, trumpet in hand. Danny was dressed for bed, striped pyjama bottoms and an Argentina jersey with 'MESSI 10' on the back. He stood in the little clearing in the living room where the other musicians were seated, laconically tuning and adjusting their instruments. Danny kept his head down and transferred his weight from foot to foot, working a kind of stage stoicism. People began to shout, 'Come on, lad!' and 'Go on, Danny!', Mark proudly trying to shush the crowd. Danny tapped his foot tentatively until the crowd noise dropped to a murmur, and with no ceremony whomped out a couple of big baggy notes, just to settle the air around him. 'Hang on, now,' he said. He set his stance again, and began to play. He waggled his shoulders in time with the music,

his cheeks inflating and hollowing, the exertions corrugat-
ing his brow, but his eyes, even as they jumped around,
maintained an ironical gaze, unimpressed and forbearing,
as if the noise filling up the room had nothing to do with
him. But he was concentrating, you could see it in his
fingers – the way they caged and danced against the trumpet's curved and tapered body, which opened out into the
startling, brassy, orchidaceous mouth of the bell.

He'd played this one before. Eileen liked it.

Tom – the man who'd come in with Murt – was standing beside Eileen, nursing a bottle of Coors. He had the
solid, weather-beaten features and wary demeanour of a
farmer on a visit to town.

'Now, that's good,' Tom said.

'He is good,' Eileen said.

'"Let's Get Lost",' Tom said.

'What?'

'The tune. "Let's Get Lost". It's by Chet Baker. That's
the good stuff, Eileen.'

'How are you finding Murt?'

'It's good to have new blood in the group. Lord knows
we need periodic freshening up.'

'Is he any good?'

'At what?'

'At the writing, I suppose.'

Tom smiled. 'I'd say Colm Tóibín won't be quaking in
his boots anytime soon. But sure look, as long as you're
getting something out of it. He's a fine young man, all
told. Getting something out of it is the main thing. That's
why the rest of us are there.'

'How long have you been in the group?'

'Oh, now. Twelve years, I'd say. We've a decent core of regulars. Adherents, like them two lunatics.' Tom nodded at the women, who were standing with Murt. The women were talking and Murt was watching them, smiling, intent. 'Other ones come and go, younger ones. Women mainly, of course. Before Murt joined there were only two regular men, myself included, and a good ten ladies. It's harder for the young to stick with things. They've other tacks to be chasing, sooner or later.'

'Twelve years,' Eileen said. 'That's a fair stint.'

'We are the terminal cases now, is what we tell ourselves. We'd a smashing woman, died of cancer coming on a year ago. She was a fine woman and she was a very gifted poet. First of the set to go. That's the joke now. We are in it to the end.'

'Sorry to hear that,' Eileen said.

'Don't be,' Tom said. 'That's life. But it doubles your resolve in some way, do you know?'

Eileen said nothing, because he didn't require an answer. Tom took a drink of his beer.

'That boy can play something beautiful. You must be proud,' Tom said, and Eileen thought that even though Danny was good, he was perhaps not so good that it merited this string of compliments. Eileen figured the man was just being agreeable, decently filling the silence, the way you had to with a stranger.

'What else would I be?' Eileen said.

# THE SILVER COAST

Lorna watched the men through the glass. The garden was covered in snow, depleted of detail and distilled to its outlines, like a sketch of a garden on tracing paper. Her husband Barry and son Luke were out there, grappling with the rust-coloured carcass of the Christmas tree Barry had finally decided to toss. It was just after one in the afternoon on a bright, cold Thursday at the tail-end of January. Lorna was standing at the kitchen counter, making coffee for the other women.

She could see the men's breaths clamouring in the air above their heads as they exerted themselves. She could see the shallow blue dimples of their prints wandering in sloppy adjacency across the snow and she could see, between their sets of prints, the jagged gutter cut by the tree's trunk and the litter of dark needles that had dropped from the tree like a line of gunpowder.

Luke, who had come to the funeral mass, was still in the charcoal overcoat his grandmother Anne had got him for his thirteenth birthday. The coat was the most grown-up piece of clothing Luke owned, but when he was in it, it only emphasised his slight shoulders and long abashed neck. There were shaggy flecks of snow clinging like burrs all up the arm and back of it

Barry was dressed like shit, in a nubbled hoodie, pulverised sweatpants and grimy Tims. He looked like someone on day release. Which in a sense he was. Barry managed the bar of the Killala Bay Hotel in town. Thursday was his day off. He tended to sleep in late, usually with a hangover, and do as little as he could get away with. Not today. As soon as they had got back to the house, Barry had been after Luke to come help him get rid of the tree.

'And every time I looked, the Being was still there,' Ciara Lavin was saying. 'If I looked away from it, I felt a sense of enormous trepidation. But whenever I looked straight back at it, the fear went away.'

Ciara Lavin was sitting at Lorna's kitchen table along with Emma Doherty and Lorna's mother, Anne. Some years ago, Ciara had travelled to South America and participated in an ayahuasca ritual. This is what she was talking about now. A guide took you into the forest and you drank a foul black liquid and hallucinated for hours, sometimes days. After she took the ayahuasca, Ciara had encountered an entity, what she called the Being, amid the trees ringing their encampment. Ciara struggled to describe the Being. It was not human but it had humanoid aspects. At times it had seemed extraterrestrial, reptilian, even machine-like. It had seemed, in some inexpressible way, feminine. It had intelligence. Ciara's sense was that the Being had a message it wanted to communicate to her, a message that Ciara intuitively understood was of the utmost importance, not just to her but to all of humanity, but she had not been equipped, or ready, to receive the message.

'You know how they say you shouldn't bore people by telling them about your dreams,' Emma Doherty said.

'Is that your way of telling me to shut up?' Ciara asked.

'It so happens I think telling people about your dreams is fine,' Emma said, 'so long as the account is brief.'

'Well it wasn't a dream,' Ciara said. 'It's silly to talk about now, but at the time it felt like the realest thing that's ever happened to me.'

'I think it sounds very fascinating,' Anne said diplomatically.

'Ayahuasca,' Emma said. 'I'm an Uisce Beatha woman myself.'

Together with Luke, the four women had just got back from the service and burial for Lydia Healy, a woman from the estate who had died suddenly a few days ago. Lydia had been in her early fifties, a good decade older than Lorna and her friends and a decade younger than Anne. None of the women had known her particularly well, but her youngest son attended the boys' secondary school with Luke, and that had been reason enough for Lorna to pay her respects. Once she had said she was going, Ciara, Emma and Anne said they would too.

Everything was close by. The service was held in the church in town, and the graveyard was only a ten-minute drive from the estate. It was another twenty-minute drive to the Silver Coast Golf Club in Enniscrone, where Lydia's family were putting on a meal for the mourners at two o'clock. The women were going to go to the golf club, but Lorna had wanted to drop Luke back first, because Luke had done his duty for the day. Luke didn't really know Mike Healy, Lydia's son, but he had come to the church anyway. Mike Healy had been a wretched sight; his body swallowed by a suit that was clearly a size too big for him. He was a bit older than Luke, fifteen or sixteen and emphatically pubescent, with scraggly porkchop sideburns and the bright red bulb of a cyst throbbing like a stalled car's warning light on the side of his nose. He had small features squished into a broad, flat face, and deep-set eyes puffy and raw with grief in a way it had been hard to look at. Lorna was proud of Luke for electing to join the line to shake the hands of the family and, when his turn came, how he had earnestly taken Mike's dazed hand in his and told him he was sorry for his loss. Returning to the house, released from the oppressive solemnity of the funeral, the women had been moved to talk, in a general and speculative way, about death. This had led to a discussion about the possibility of an afterlife, which had led to a discussion concerning planes of existence, which had led to Ciara sitting here relating her experience with the Being in a South American forest.

Lorna plunged the press and brought the coffee over to the kitchen table.

'I've no decent biscuits, I'm afraid,' she said.

'Stop,' Anne said.

'Imagine if coffee tasted as good as it actually smelled,' Emma said, pouring herself a cup.

'How are the two men faring?' Emma asked Lorna.

'I think Barry's after knocking Luke over. There's snow all up his coat.'

Anne got up off her chair and went over to the window.

'He'll have that poor lad's coat ruined,' Anne said. 'And where exactly is he going with that tree?'

Lorna joined Anne.

'I would wager he's going to dump it in the ditch at the back of the estate,' Lorna said.

'Why wouldn't he just leave it out for the binmen?'

'That's not the way Barry's mind works. For weeks I've been telling him to leave the tree out and he wouldn't lift a finger. Until –' Lorna spread her hands in exasperation '– he decides this morning the tree has to go *right now*, and that's that. The collection's not till Monday but all of a sudden it can't wait.'

Lorna and Anne watched Barry drop the tree, knock open the gate at the back of the garden, then work it out into the alley behind the house.

'They are making some operation of it, all right,' Anne said.

'There's this idea, that men were more capable back in the day,' Emma said. 'Would you say that's true, Anne?'

'Are you saying my men are incapable?' Lorna interjected.

'No more than mine!' Emma said.

'It's hard to know,' Anne said. 'You see all types, and then you see them come back around again.'

'Daddy wasn't like that,' Lorna said.

'Wasn't like what?' Anne asked.

'Like, impetuous . . .' Lorna said, reluctant now to talk Barry down even though he deserved it.

'Oh, your daddy had his moments too,' Anne said.

Barry and Luke had left the gate open behind them. It drifted on its hinges.

'Here's a question, Anne,' Emma snapped brightly. 'What's your earliest memory?'

'My earliest memory. Oh, now, nothing special.'

'But as a kid,' Emma insisted.

The Dohertys had moved into the estate two years back, which made Emma the newest member of Lorna's circle. Quickly, Emma had positioned herself as the talker, the coaxer. No one was allowed to be quiet in her presence. She went after anyone reticent, anyone attempting to hold their counsel, as if continually cornering others might forestall her ever being cornered herself.

'Summer, I'd say,' Anne said, after thinking about it. 'Out on the lake with my brothers and sisters.'

'That's what everyone remembers,' Lorna said. 'Summer.'

'I remember looking at the little chewed-up spot on my mam's arm from her inoculation shot, and wondering what on earth that was. One time I asked her, and she said, "That's from where you bit me as a babby. You tried to run away on me," she told me, "and when I caught up with you, you bit me on the arm." That's what she said. That's what I remember.'

'And do you remember when Lorna was little?' Emma asked.

'Of course! Like yesterday.'

'And what was she like?'

Anne looked at her daughter. 'Oh, now. She was the same.'

'Now that I don't know how to take,' Lorna said.

'It's the way time goes,' Anne said. 'It becomes all of a piece.'

'I didn't mean to do down your men,' Emma said to Lorna, suddenly contrite.

'You're forgiven,' Lorna said.

Lorna was thinking about Lydia Healy. The woman had taken ill in the supermarket. Heart attack. Word was she had died in the frozen-food aisle, right next to a bin of cut-price Christmas hams the supermarket was selling off before they went out of date. That's what people were saying, anyway. In her mind Lorna was able to picture the scene with an omniscient minuteness of detail – Lydia Healy down on her back on the filthy, sticky supermarket linoleum, trolley askew in the aisle, the teenage staff in their short-sleeve polyester work shirts gathering around her, stricken and incredulous as Lydia gasped for breath. The indignity of it.

Lorna believed she had seen a man die once, at a beach resort, as a teenager. Lorna, her mother and her father, Tom, were on holiday in Nice with Auntie Moira and Lorna's cousins. A man had taken gravely ill on the beach, a few yards from them. Lorna could not say for sure that he was gone by the time the paramedics strapped him to a gurney and carried him up the beach, but she was convinced she had seen him pass the threshold beyond which there was no coming back. She remembers children screaming ecstatically and inflatables bobbing in the surf like bright trash, and further out the clenched shoulders of adults as they waded beyond the bearably waist-high waves. Lorna had been Luke's age, thirteen, fourteen, and the man had seemed very old, though he was probably only in his early fifties. He was with a woman, presumably his wife. The wife was sitting on a towel with her knees drawn up to her bust and they were arguing in the injurious, teacherly cadences of the well-off British. The woman wanted to leave. The man said something about going back in the water. *You do what you want to do, Margaret*, Lorna remembers the man saying, and she could still hear him now, more than twenty years on, the low, patient note of deeply grooved spite in his voice. *You always get to do exactly what you want to do.* He was standing over the woman, and after a little while, he abruptly stopped his jeering and sat down on the towel next to hers, as if the argument was over. Then, in Lorna's memory, the man looked straight at her – at teenage Lorna. His mouth was ajar, and he wore a puzzled, mildly stunned expression, like a man on a train platform who at the very last moment delays for some unaccountable fraction and must watch the carriage doors seal shut right in front of his nose. He wasn't going anywhere; it was all at once going away from him.

'Do you remember in Nice,' Lorna began, 'Mam? Remember the beach in Nice when that man died right in front of everyone.'

'What?' Anne said.

'We were on holiday with Moira and a man died on the beach right in front of us.'

Lorna knew by her mother's expression that she had no idea what Lorna was talking about.

'You don't remember? How could you not remember someone dying?' Lorna said.

'I remember ... someone having an issue, an allergic

reaction? I thought maybe it was a woman, though. And it wasn't in Nice.'

'But you remember going on holiday in Nice with Auntie Moira? I was Luke's age.'

'I do.'

'Well, there you go,' Lorna said. 'We – well, *I* saw a man drop dead on the beach there.'

Through the window Lorna could see Barry and Luke coming back up the garden. Barry slid open the patio door and the two stepped inside and began stamping their feet on the mat, the cold that came in with them spreading like a clear thought in the warm room.

'I think we better be going if we want to make this lunch,' Ciara said.

'Isn't it an awful thing,' Emma said. 'Someone dies on you and you have to make sure everyone gets fed.'

'Did you even talk to this one when she was alive?' Barry asked Lorna.

'I talked to her. I talked to her on several occasions,' Lorna said, though this was barely true; fleeting exchanges in the school hallways at parent–teacher nights, a two-minute chat at a christening or backyard get-together.

'Can't say I was left with much of an impression of her,' Barry said.

'Where's that tree gone?' Lorna asked him.

'You know where it's gone.'

The north-west corner of the estate boundaried a flank of Belleek Woods, and the alley behind the house led right into the screened clearing just beyond the treeline. Vagrants sometimes slept there, teenagers drank there, and some of the more indifferent households – and Barry's actions meant Lorna's household now numbered among them – occasionally used it as a dumping site.

'You shouldn't be throwing stuff back there.'

'That tree is nature,' Barry said. He scratched his cheek and smiled complacently at his wife. He looked at his shoe and with a delicate sliding motion eased a final tuft of snow from the edge of his boot on to the mat.

'Is there any coffee left?' he asked.

'There's a drop there,' Lorna said. 'I'd make more but we're off to the meal in the Silver Coast.'

'Shite! Grub. Maybe I'll come so!' said Barry. 'I'm starved.'

Luke had taken off his coat. As he was trying to hang it up, Anne intercepted him and began batting the snow-flecked sleeve.

'Where's your hat gone?' Anne asked him. Then, to Lorna, 'Did this man not have a hat at the funeral?'

'I think I ... left it in Mam's car,' Luke said uncertainly.

'If you've lost that hat, Luke,' Lorna said.

'I'm pretty sure it's in the car,' Luke said.

'Hats, gloves, scarves, glasses. He puts them down for a split second and that's that, you never see them again. It's a kind of gift he has,' Lorna said.

'You missed Ciara here telling us about the fiend she met in the woods in Peru off her head on drugs,' Emma told Barry.

'Did I,' Barry said absently, pouring the last of the coffee into a cup.

'It wasn't a fiend,' Ciara said. 'It was a Being.'

The women had moved into the hallway and were putting back on their coats.

Barry followed them out, sipping at his coffee.

'Aren't you all good neighbours, all the same,' he declared.

'There's nothing wrong with being civil,' Anne said.

'What'll me and Luke do for lunch?' Barry asked Lorna.

Lorna opened the front door and stood side-on to let the other women leave first. She reached into her coat pocket expecting to find her car keys there, but they weren't, which meant she must have left them in the ignition.

'I'm sure you can fend for yourselves,' she told her husband.

Lorna was sitting alone at a table in the dining room of the Silver Coast clubhouse. Ciara and Emma had drifted away into the crowd. Anne had returned to the buffet for another cup of tea. The edges of the room thrummed with a tentative liveliness, people walking around exchanging guarded smiles.

At the far end of Lorna's table an elderly woman was supping on a bowl of vegetable soup the colour and consistency of phlegm. The woman had neither spoken to or acknowledged Lorna and was concentrating entirely on her soup. In front of Lorna was a ham and coleslaw sandwich, soggy in the centre and cardboardy along the crusts. She'd managed one bite and didn't have the stomach for the rest. It felt wrong to just abandon the sandwich. It felt disrespectful, and though she knew no one present would care whether she finished this little bit of food, the thought she could not dispel from her mind was that Lydia Healy would care. That if some remnant of Healy had survived her death, that remnant was surely here, present in the air of the Silver Coast clubhouse, watching the afternoon unfold. This thought unnerved Lorna, not because it was in any way something she believed but because its continued intrusion in her mind reminded her that she had not particularly liked Lydia Healy, that, finite as their contact had been, she had nonetheless found something lurking and coldly aloof in Healy's manner and bearing, the way she bluntly avoided eye contact and seemed to speak only in curt, defensive remarks.

Lorna saw her mother coming through the crowd. With a sidelong glance at the woman eating soup, Lorna hastily slipped what was left of the sandwich into a napkin, transferred the napkin into her coat pocket and rose from the table. She met Anne in the middle of the room.

'I need some air, I think.'

'Oh, OK,' Anne replied. 'What about my tea?'

'Stay and have it if you want, or bring it.'

They walked out across the links. The sandy cavities of the bunkers were lightly dusted with snow and looked phosphorescent. The snow on the open stretches of fairway grass, exposed to the wind slicing in off the sea, had settled in nervous patches. The wind was like ice. Lorna folded her arms tight to her body as she walked.

'Where do you want to go?' Anne asked.

'Are your hands not freezing?' Lorna asked. Her mother's hands were ungloved and exposed. Anne had brought her tea – a ceramic cup and saucer – with her.

'They feel like they're burning,' Anne said.

She took a sup of the tea and tossed the dregs. They were passing a putting green with a hole and a flag sticking out of it. Anne detoured on to the green and set the cup and saucer down by the hole.

'Remind me to get that on the way back,' she said. 'Speaking of which, did you find Luke's hat?'

'In the car? I forgot to check,' Lorna admitted. From the vantage of the links, the sea looked to Lorna like a vast, pitted slab of vitreous dark blue rock, like something that, once you reached it, you could walk right out on to.

'We'll go as far as we can,' she said, 'and when we get back, I think it'll be time to leave.'

They followed one of the improvised trails that led off the links, down between a gap in the sand dunes. There was no one else on the strand, the surf a sickly yellow foam bubbling between the matted black hanks of seaweed heaped on the beach. Lorna had to screw her eyes against the grains of sand zinging through the air.

'What *did* you make of Lydia Healy?' she asked her mother.

'Well now,' Anne said, folding her own arms against herself, 'I don't think I knew her enough to form a meaningful impression.'

Lorna glanced at Anne.

'That's an excessively careful way of putting it.'

'I do have a story.'

'Oh.'

'It's a little story. It's nothing scandalous.'

'Go on.'

'In fact it's not even a story. There was just this . . . moment.' She shook her head. 'It was Bonnie Walshe's wedding, you remember the reception was at the Pontoon Hotel back when the Pontoon was still open? This must have been a good ten years back. Do you want to hear this?'

'If there's scandal.'

'I told you there's no scandal.'

'Tell me what you're going to tell me,' Lorna said.

'We were in the middle of the dinner and I got a work call. The reception was cat so I had to go all the way outside. When I step back in, I'm making my way down the hall to the little lobby, which I can see is empty but for Lydia Healy, stood up at the reception desk with her back to me. There was no one at the desk and I figure, well, she's rung the bell and she's just waiting for someone to come out to her. Next thing, though, Lydia takes a look one way, then the other and darts in behind the desk and starts rifling through whatever's behind there. I can't see because the counter was blocking, but whatever she was looking for she was looking for it very methodically and very urgently.'

'What was she doing? Was she looking for money?' Lorna asked.

'I don't think they keep money behind the reception desk; even ten years ago almost everyone was paying by card. I always thought she must have been looking for keys to a room.'

'Why? To take something from one of the rooms? Maybe she was—' Lorna was going to say 'having an affair'. Waiting for the reception desk to be unmanned, then grabbing a key card for an illicit quickie with her lover. But this was a preposterous scenario. Lydia Healy? Having a tumultuous affair? A woman who, when you looked at her, made you think of terms like *beetling* and *doughty*, words that were archaic and obscure and cumbersome and probably didn't even mean what you thought they meant.

'Maybe she was a kleptomaniac,' Lorna suggested instead. 'Stealing just to steal. Saw a chance and couldn't help herself.'

'I don't know if she even took anything from the desk,' Anne said. 'I was coming down the hall and she looked up. It was too late for me to turn back. She saw me coming and she must have been thinking, *that's it, I'm caught*, only I was too embarrassed to say anything so I lowered my eyes and just walked on by like she wasn't there . . . She ended up in a group I was chatting with later that night and of course she acted, and I acted, like nothing had happened.'

'What else could you do?'

'Anyway. That's all there was to that story. But that was the first thing that came to mind when you asked me what I thought about poor Lydia Healy, God rest her.'

The women stopped walking. Ahead of them a couple of gulls were picking their way through the surf, long yellow beaks jabbing at the sand. One of them flashed the amber bead of its reptilian eye in the direction of the women and flounced its wings, once, a single pronounced *whump*.

'They are some size, actually,' Anne said.

'I know.'

'Once you get up close. They're the size of dogs.'

'Descended from dinosaurs,' Lorna said.

She remembered the sandwich in her pocket.

'Probably, there's a completely mundane explanation

for what Lydia Healy was up to behind that desk,' she said as she unwrapped the sandwich from the napkin and tore the remains into chunks. 'Only we don't know it.'

'The world is full of unaccountable things, if you're keeping track,' Anne said.

'And who keeps track?' Lorna asked as she lobbed a bread chunk. The gulls began tearing at the morsel with violent enthusiasm.

'Can they eat that?' Anne asked. 'The ham and the cole-slaw and all that?'

'They can eat anything, I think.'

Lorna tossed the rest of the sandwich. She and her mother watched the gulls until they were finished, then they turned and began to make their way back towards the Silver Coast.

# ANHEDONIA, HERE I COME

BOBBY TALLIS possessed the drainpipe physique, knee-length mackintosh, and balefully frail demeanour of a poet, or so he believed, as he pursued a lavishly wayward course across the mangy municipal parks, median strips and depressed residential quadrangles of his quarter of the city on another blustery October afternoon. One hand broodingly ensconced within a pocket, Bobby smoked as he walked and made rapid, furtive motions with his lips, as if in intense, collusive conversation with himself. Bobby *was* a poet.

He lived in a dilapidated apartment block on the south-side inner city, a block so populated with retirees and pensioners that visitors – of which Bobby had absolutely none – often mistook it for a state retirement home. Bobby was certain he was the only resident under the age of sixty. The block's corridors – the sour-cream walls lit by low-wattage sconces downy with dust; the furred, blue, perpetually damp carpeting in which shoe-print impressions dolefully lingered – evoked for Bobby a budget version of the afterlife. It was, at least, a peaceful place, no noise but the late-night dysphagic judders of the lift's recurringly jammed doors.

Bobby walked six miles every day. He did so because a lengthy walk helped oxygenate the creative capacities as well as pre-emptively dispel the oppressive sense of cabin fever that would consume him if he did not regularly remove himself from the tiny tomb of his one-bedroom apartment. Also, there was a shopping-centre car park three miles from his building where he bought weed from a schoolgirl on a near-daily basis.

The city was bound on this side by a canal, and Bobby's peregrinations tended to bring him, as now, into intermittent contact with this body of water. He noted the tarry density of its bilious murk, the tidemark of pearlescent scum bearding the centuries-old brickwork as the canal subsided towards the stark quays and the notional sea beyond. Bobby traversed the back lane of a housing estate and detoured through a brushy interval that served as one of the numerous pickup sites scattered across this side of the city – with a grin he registered the dangling lobe of a used condom snagged on the branch of a bush like a dismal festive decoration. He stopped at a McDonald's drive-through, inhaled three one-euro hamburgers, a fries and a Coke, and took a spumous dump in a toilet cubicle bathed in the purple-blue glow of anti-injection UV lighting.

In the bathroom mirror Bobby studied himself.

With his cheeks flocked with old acne scars, the sebum gleam of his forehead, his significant but gracefully tapering nose (his favourite feature), inexpiably seedy smile, and untameable squall of dark curls, Bobby, at twenty-nine, resembled a not unhandsome but grotesquely ancient teen-ager, a physical template he considered not unsuitable for a poet. Adolescence was the stage of human development at which nostalgia (that is, the awareness of mortality) first becomes fatally possible, and was the reft, the fracture, out of which poetry grows. The greatest poets, so Bobby believed, lived and died without losing the furious unrea-son, self-consuming nerviness and malign naivety of teenagerhood.

He washed his hands with pink chemical soap and resumed his walk.

He wanted to be a poet but suffered from a day job, or at least a source of regular income, that was at this stage a discipline almost as interesting: he was a popular house art-ist on the online-community site AllFreeekArt, confecting pornographic paintings and animated shorts according to the punctilious specifications of a zealously loyal and stead-ily expanding client base. He drew Disney princesses, anthropomorphised ponies, superheroes, video-game pro-tagonists and cartoon versions of celebrities in endless combinations of graphic congress. His clients craved every conventional iteration of the erotically depictable, but the medium of animation also permitted the realisation of dimensions, stylisations and acts not available to reality, and Bobby enjoyed the challenge of actualising the more out-landish of the carnal vistas sweated up by his customers. Towards those most recherché of deviants, the real sickos, Bobby felt something close to affection. As he absorbed their anguishedly detailed requests, he realised that the purest perverts longed for their own species of the poetic, for the incarnation of the inconsummatable.

These clients were also willing to pay the most. By this point, from his drawings animation, Bobby was making something perilously close to a living. The money came into his bank account, and then came in again, like a tide. He withdrew only the minimum necessary. A healthy surplus was building and it disquieted him how much the money consoled him. He did not want to believe in it yet felt a swell of relief each time he thought of it. Enough money meant you did not have to think about money.

Then there were the poems. Bobby had been writing and rewriting and refining and re-refining the manuscript of his debut collection for more than eight years now. The collection was currently entitled *Anhedonia, Here I Come*. He regularly read from this endless work in progress at open-mic nights, had even had a few of the poems published in double-digit-circulation pamphlets and once reputable, now posthumous journals. The poems, he suspected, were not good enough. They exhibited decent technical effects but were in some obscure way insubstantial or evasive. He agonised over the accuracy of his inner ear, was not in fact certain he even possessed one. In terms of theme, he could not get beyond what he was convinced was a fundamentally spurious obsession with suicidal ideation, but simultaneously he felt that every other poetic topic or concern was an obfuscation, an eschewal, or a bald retreat from this theme.

Bobby had been smitten with the concept of suicide since he was a teenager, but the problem, he figured, was that he had never truly wished to kill himself. His basic problem was that he liked being alive. Being alive was, if not the best thing, then at least an OK thing, an endlessly

OK thing. Much as he wished otherwise, Bobby had gradually come to accept that he was afflicted with an uncapsizable psycho-chemical equilibrium, and no matter how much squalor and degradation he encountered, no matter how many ill-considered partners he initiated relationships with, and no matter how many drugs he crammed into his system, he could not jar himself into a genuine spiral. Not being able to feel crushingly terrible made him feel terrible, but even this second order of terribleness had, to his inquisitive mind, a compelling textural quality that made him wish only to experience more of it: his mind found any sensation or state induced by it fascinating, which was an indirect way of admitting that his mind found *itself* fascinating, which was to say that he, Bobby Tallis, found every facet of his own disgustingly mundane self and life fascinating. Bobby's psychic sturdiness was, he feared, a manifestation of a submerged but profound and pullulating narcissism.

Still, duty-bound as a poet, Bobby diligently wondered about mortality and the volitional ending of a life: specifically your own. He figured that you did not want to kill yourself because you felt bad, because if you felt bad you perforce retained access to a spectrum of emotional feeling on which was located the possibility of one day again, however provisionally, feeling *good*. You wanted to kill yourself, Bobby suspected, only when the access to any feeling at all, whether good or bad, was completely eroded, when you found yourself, as many poor souls did, mired upon an undifferentiatedly flat and horizonless plane of Unfeeling, bereft of access to any avenue of actual or potential emotional excitation. It was not Feeling that killed but the final and irremediable withdrawal of it. Bobby had read the literature. This state, he knew, was called anhedonia.

Moving through the moulting trees, Bobby saw the beige-coloured brutalist slab of the shopping centre climb into the skyline. His dealer he knew only by her first name, Becky. She was a convent schoolgirl and camogie player. She often brought her stick and gear bag with her and sold little ten-spots of reliably mediocre weed in a corner of the car park most afternoons. A small coven of teammates tended to tag along, hanging back in mute judgement, no doubt, of Becky's clientele.

Bobby pounded across the car park and instantly discerned Becky in her green uniform, another person with her. Empty plastic bags stirred in the breeze. They lifted and settled, flinched like dying nerves as Bobby tramped on them: the sky itself was the colour of a shopping bag. A rat, a sliver of dark muscle, darted across the concrete and vanished into the crumbling base of a low stone wall.

The other person was a man with a baby strapped like a bomb to his chest in an impressive-looking harness. Becky's camán-wielding cohort lounged on the stone wall, observing the exchange with studied wrath. Bobby held up between a couple of cars. He watched the transaction. Becky giggled, discreetly palmed the man a baggie as she pulled a funny face and patted the baby on the head. The harnessed baby's loose limbs waggled and its head bobbled disinterestedly around. Bobby thought of a trussed crab unaware it is about to be boiled alive. He picked his nose, unseated a gratifyingly intact clump of dried matter, palpated it between his fingers, and flicked it away. The

man – youngish, with shaved blond hair – walked across
the car park and placed first the child and then himself
into a gleaming hypertrophied Land Rover. Bobby now
approached.

'All right, Becky.'

Becky grimaced and flexed the wings of her nose. 'The
usual, Bob?'

'Becky, can I ask—'

'No.'

'Can I ask is Becky your real name?'

'Why would Becky not be my real name?'

'Cos I wouldn't use my real name, if I were you. I'd
deploy an alias, if I were you.'

'An alias?'

'Do you know what that is?'

She sighed.

'I know what an alias is, you horse's arse. Stop being
predatory.'

'Predatory?'

'You're initiating predatory behaviour. Don't think I
won't bash your balls in with my camogie.'

'Aaaay!' her friends on the wall cheered derisively.

'I'm not— OK. Jesus Christ. Can I just get my stuff?'

'The usual?'

'The usual.'

'Big spender,' she said as she palmed him the ten-spot.
'This is it, I think, Bob. This is the last time I'm serving you.'

'Listen, if it's about asking your real name, I'm sorry, I
didn't mean—'

She jerked her shoulder, indicated the lumpy appur-
tenance of her camogie bag. Her helmet, with its white

dome and ribbed face guard, rocked against her hip. It looked like the skull of a vanquished opponent she had taken as a war trophy.

'The school got to the county quarters for the first time in twelve years or some bullshit. We're doubling down on training sessions for the foreseeable future. And anyway. I been doing *this* –' she indicated the car park '– like, two years now. It has a built-in lifespan, Bob. Might be time to get out of the game.'

'The game? But what about the money? Won't you miss the money?' Bobby asked.

'I don't do this for the money, Bob. I do it because it's interesting. But now it's time to, I dunno, grow up or whatever.'

Now Bobby grimaced. 'Don't do that, Becky.'

She looked at him again. She had a broad frame and dimpled knees, a clearwater complexion and streaked, tawny-brown hair. Bobby considered her – considered her in a rigorously paternalistic way – very beautiful. For the first time he could recall, something in her expression softened.

'There's Mike Logan? You know him? He's got the old school tattoos, naked ladies with their boobs out and every-thing, all up his arms?'

'Mike sounds like a character.'

'That he is,' Becky replied. 'He's sound. He hangs out in the bookie's on Hyde Street, Bob. He can sort you out from now on. I'm happy to vouch as to the quality of his merchandise. And I can vouch on your behalf to him.'

'Don't take this the wrong way, Becky, but it's you I'll miss.'

'Ah ah ah,' she said, wagging an admonishing finger like a mother scolding an errant toddler. 'Goodbye, Bob. And if you see me again, cross the fucking street, right?'

'Goodbye, Becky,' he said.

She turned and went to her friends. They unsaddled themselves from the wall and the group headed out on to the main street. Feeling woozily, torrentially fifteen himself, Bobby stood there with the ten-spot crushed in his hot grip and a corona of flush diffusing across his pocked cheeks as he waited to see if the girl he'd known as Becky would at least look back.

The Land Rover nearly struck him as he wafted towards the shopping-centre exit. He stood in place in order to let the monstrosity eke by, but instead it eased to a halt and the passenger window slid down. As Bobby looked in, he caught the man hastily sucking in his gut before leaning across the latte-coloured leather of the passenger seat. It was the man with the baby Becky had served before Bobby.

'I thought I recognised you,' the man said.

'Huh?' Bobby said.

'I was at one of the reading nights at the Andromeda bar, like a month ago. I saw you read. You were good.' When Bobby did not respond the guy lowered his eyes and said, with the grave deprecation of a bad actor, 'I mean – you wouldn't have known I was there. Not that it matters if you did.'

Then he looked up and smiled. Bobby stared at his teeth, which were neatly aligned and all the same, toothpaste-ad hue. He *appeared* to be nothing more than a nondescriptly handsome wodge of heteronormative generica, tidily style-less in a sweater and chinos, but his dopily enthused expression was so innocuous it was unnerving. And Bobby felt, unmistakably, an emanation, the old encoded carnal pang, the way the air tautens right before a sudden burst of rain. He uptilted his nose to signify scepticism, and also because he believed this angle resolved the geometry of his face into its most attractive configuration.

'A lot of people come to those things. Actually, that's not true. Barely anyone comes. But yeah, if you say you were there. Well. Good for you.'

'It's an interesting scene.'

'It's interesting if you're into it.'

'But it's impressive. Getting up there and actually doing it.'

'Anyone can,' Bobby said. The baby in the rear of the Land Rover made a noise. 'That your baby?'

The man shifted in his seat. 'Oh, uh. Oh no.'

'That's a disconcerting answer.'

The man's grin broke. He reached into the back and grasped the baby's foot. 'I look after the kid. It's my job, sort of. This is my half-sister, Saoirse.'

'Saoirse get high with you or what, then?'

'Well—' The man blushed. 'No, but she's a good accomplice, ha-ha.' He actually said 'ha-ha'. 'She keeps quiet about these clandestine little runs we make.'

'I see,' Bobby said. Another moment passed. A ragged silence settled between the two men. If one of them did not offer something in the next few seconds, the conversation, such as it was, would die. Bobby stymied an inner disgust, sighed, and said his three least favourite words in the world.

'Do you write?'

Bobby saw it straight away: the fretful, eager, abashed flinch and bristle.

'Uh, I mean, I'm trying,' the man admitted. 'I mean, I'm not any good.'

'You'd fit right in, then,' Bobby said. 'At the Andromeda.'

'No, man, you're on another level to what I'm doing.'

Bobby shrugged. 'There's always more levels.' He removed his hand from his pocket, the baggie dangling between his fingers. 'Now, if you'll excuse me. I need to go get lightly spaced.'

The guy lunged at the passenger door, pushed it open. 'Look, I detained you enough to offer you a lift at least, if you want.'

Bobby looked into the interior of the car, the guy watching him, waiting.

'I see,' Bobby said.

The guy's head came swimming up out of Bobby's lap after a long minute of strenuous and sudsy fellatio. He blinked like a man who has just been jarred from a deep dream, eyes bloodshot and tear-filmed. He put his forearm up to his humid mouth, seemed to sink his teeth into his flesh, and made an anguished noise.

'Hey, hey, it's OK,' Bobby said.

'I'm just – I can't with the kid here.'

'Yeah . . .' Bobby turned his head and saw the flesh-toned distortion of his own face floating in the rectangle of black glass partitioning the back of the vehicle's interior from the front. As Bobby did up his fly the guy brought the partition back down. A nursery-pop jingle was burbling gently from the rear speakers. The baby had taken

hold of one of her legs and was trying to guide her fat foot
into her mouth, an activity she now suspended in order to
smile very prettily at her half-sibling's blotchy, remorseful
face.

'It was kind of weirding me out too,' Bobby lied.

'I'm sorry, I'm sorry,' the guy said. 'This isn't how I pic-
tured my afternoon.'

'You're all right,' Bobby said, suddenly wary. The key
now was to get out before the guy started unloading about
his originary trauma or whatever.

'It's my father – he'll, he'll throw me out on the street
again if he finds out I did something like this – in his car –
with Saoirse right fucking there! Jesus! Jesus!'

Bobby glanced at his phone. Two missed calls and a text,
all from Fiachra Calhoun. The text simply said *In Andromeda*. Normally, Bobby would have ignored or evaded
Calhoun's midweek-afternoon overtures, but right now he
needed a drink.

'Listen, I got to go,' he said.

'My fucking father, man,' the guy said. 'I'm sorry to
drag you into this.'

'You're not dragging me into anything,' Bobby assured
him. They were parked in an alley. Bobby quickly tried the
passenger-door handle. The vehicle was centrally locked.
'I do have to go, though.'

The guy sighed again. 'Fuckit.' He reached across Bobby
and popped the glove compartment. He took out a small
wallet and removed from that a baggie of powder. Nipped
it open, licked and dipped a finger, ran the finger round his
gums. Then he eyed Bobby again. 'Want a bump?' he said
in a choked tone.

'I'm absolutely good. Let me out. Please.'

The guy looked confused, even injured, for a moment. Then he pressed the relevant button.

'Wait, wait, wait,' he said as Bobby stepped with relief into the alley. 'I know I've fucked this up. But I wanted to see if I could show you some of my work. Could you do that? Could you look at it for me?'

He held up his phone. 'Can I just get, like, your email or maybe a followback?'

'I only edit hard copy,' Bobby said.

'I'll print it off and send it to you,' he said, holding Bobby's eye with a kind of ruthless helplessness.

Bobby felt the warmth of burdenhood settle on him as he spelled out his address.

'Poems?' Bobby asked.

The guy shook his head. 'Some poems. There's some stories too. What I need to know about is the sentences. I just want to know if they are doing something interesting or not.'

'I can't help myself. I don't know how I can help you.'

'You can, you can.'

The guy dipped, ran another dab of whatever was in the baggie around his mouth. He was, Bobby had to admit, an intriguing mess. He had no doubt the guy would send him his stuff and Bobby already knew he would instantly junk it and flag the guy's mails as spam. The guy insisted on shaking hands before allowing Bobby to walk off.

As he emerged from the mouth of the alley, Bobby checked his messages. Then he realised he was abandoning an infant to a vehicle under the operation of a man kneading tinctures of a patently illicit substance into his

face. Bobby turned and looked back and waited to see if
there was anything obvious he could rebuke himself for
not doing. The vehicle began to move. He watched it
complete a spasmodic reverse and trundle towards the far
opening of the alley. Then it was gone.

Fiachra Calhoun was in his customary nook at the rear of
the Andromeda, which at this hour was near-empty. Jess
Tombes was with him.

Fiachra's resting posture was raked-in and inert, like the
heap of cinders left after a fire has gone out. Bobby knew
Fiachra took on this appearance of incinerated introversion
only when he was absolutely blitzed. Sober, or moderately
soused, he was an animate, wryly handsome 52-year-old
poet, essayist and workshop leader, and the senior editor at,
in Bobby's opinion, the country's sole remotely respectable
poetry publishing house. Hammered, he looked two hundred. He raised his ashen lids and grinned wobblingly at
Bobby.

'How is the man?' he said.

'Well,' Bobby said.

'Hey,' Jess said.

Jess had a straight fringe and pristine, unreadable blue
eyes. She was in college and served as a kind of all-purpose
intern-slash-assistant to Fiachra. She was writing poems,
of course. She was sitting with one leg tucked under her
on a battered leather chair and appeared to be stone sober.

'What's happening, Fiachra?'

'Ach, we're celebrating.'

'Just the two of you?'

'Well, there's three of us now,' Jess said.

'What are we celebrating?'

'It's a dismal Wednesday afternoon, yet we have warmth, seats, wine and friends,' Fiachra said. 'And someone's wrote a book.'

'Everyone's written a book,' Bobby said, but as he did his heart spasmed fretfully in its chamber.

'Congratulate Miss Tombes,' Fiachra said. 'We're putting her out next spring.'

Jess glanced down into her drink. Bobby had an immediate urge to punch both of them in the face.

'That's. Great. That's. So. Great,' Bobby heard himself incontinently reiterate.

Jess Tombes. Jess Tombes. Who and what, exactly, was Jess Tombes? Bobby logged what he knew of her: a student, a kid, she was an unfailingly polite and pleasant human, conscientious, patient, and kind with anyone she encountered, so it seemed. She formed rapports easily, and – a rarity in the scene – Bobby had yet to encounter someone willing to say a bad word about her. She was writing, but had been purportedly reluctant to show the poems to others. (Bobby had offered to critique them, more than once.) He'd heard her read a couple of them one night. They'd been pretty good, actually, maybe, he thought now.

Bobby's head swam, tritely. It wasn't even a question of whether or not she was objectively better than him, it's that Fiachra had thought so, and soon others would too. Fiachra had published a number of individual pieces by Bobby over the years in various journals and anthologies, had put him in every live-reading line-up going. Not that he thought he'd be Fiachra's next guy, necessarily – he just wished now that it was anyone other than the baby-faced Tombes. (Though he knew that this qualification, too, was a lie. He would envy and despise all who were not he, if he was not the one.)

'We signed off on the contracts in the office at noon. Been here since. Good that we could rely on at least one layabout to answer the call to quietly celebrate,' Fiachra said.

For the next ten minutes or so, Bobby interacted. He choked out questions, smiled, and nodded meaningfully at replies. He was trying to interpret Fiachra's tone – whether it contained a buried note of contrition or at least an awareness of his having, from Bobby's perspective, rejected him for Jess. There was the gruesome possibility that Fiachra simply expected Bobby to take developments at face value, and be happy for Tombes. Bobby excused himself. In the toilet he closed his fist, hyperventilated, and punched the metal hand-dryer. He looked at his hand. He was pretty convinced he had broken something in his middle finger, through which a steady and piercing voltage of pain now vibrantly coursed. Bobby went back out and drank five pints. Fiachra, with a significant head start but still intent on trying to keep up, rapidly became unintelligible, then unconscious. Jess ordered during each round, bought her own, yet seemed to sit before the same glass of wine drained to the same unvarying depth all night long.

'Do you feel good?' Bobby asked for what felt like the hundredth time, though it may have been the first time he had actually said it out loud to her.

Jess took her time before answering, as she took her

time before answering any question. She was looking at him, and he was looking at her, and she was looking at him looking at her. There she sat, twenty-one or twenty-two, icily wreathed in all her untradable surplus time, watching not just Bobby and Fiachra but also somehow herself, insinuated within yet in some way already beyond – already extricated from – this scene, this moment. Bobby could see now the abiding apartness in her look. It had always been there. And within him rose again the habitual suspicion, the deep intestinal hunch: his work was shit. Rich, black, viscous, tarry shit. So, essentially, was Fiachra's, and everybody else's. But Tombes's, whatever it was, was not. Jess Tombes was going to last, and Bobby could feel himself, in her spectral, incipiently canonical gaze, being transubstantiated, molecule by molecule, into obscurity. Whether she knew it or not – and Bobby hazarded she probably did not – she was killing them all so that she could go on, so that she could make it. This was how the machine worked.

'I do,' she said in a voice so low it sounded as if it was coming from inside Bobby's own skull.

He looked at his phone. It was getting late. The bar had filled up. He wanted to cry. He put his hand on Jess's knee. She looked at his hand.

'What is that?' she asked.

'I don't know,' Bobby said. He withdrew the still aching hand, yawned, closed his eyes, and pinched tears from his lashes. He was very, very drunk. 'I am very, very drunk,' he announced.

Fiachra was snoring, head back against his seat. Bobby wanted to ball up his mackintosh and smother him with it, he wanted to rouse Fiachra and beg him, with tears in his eyes, *pick me, pick me.*

Jess reached for a beer mat, and Bobby watched her place it down in almost but not quite the same spot. The discrepancy, or adjustment, was deliberate. Everything she did was deliberate and precise. She was editing, fixing, curating this moment, as if it was already an old, old memory she was coaxing back to life. And Bobby felt like – nothing, like some wavering and indistinct presence cluttering up the dimmest margins of that memory, some smudgily recalled minor character she might leave in for the sake of texturing, or just cut altogether, when she was writing this scene out, however many years from now, sitting at a desk in a huge stone house deep in the woods at dusk, the rambunctious squawking and chirping of starlings reverberating in the eaves and the warm, drunken laughter of friends drifting temptingly from the garden below, ready to call it a day on the day's writing but not just yet as she earnestly attempted to remember, *what even was that arsehole's name?*

Bobby stood up.

'I'm so glad for you,' he managed, and he walked right out.

First he saw the pale humps, then he saw what they were. Old people, huddled on the pavement and some seated or even lying on the grassy embankment outside the apartment block. Some were in pyjamas, some in overcoats, some with their blankets draped over their shoulders. A young man and a young woman were moving alertly from person to person, talking to them and gesturing reassuringly.

As Bobby staggered up to the building entrance, the

young man jogged over. He had a denim shirt on with the
sleeves rolled capably up.

'What's up?' Bobby asked mildly.

'Gas leak.'

'Extremely potentially dangerous!' the young woman,
joining him, exclaimed.

Bobby ignored them. He took out his key and went to
open the door into the foyer.

'The gas company said to stay out of the building!' the
young man said. 'No unlocking doors and no naked flames
inside or in the vicinity of the building.'

'The fire brigade is on the way,' the young woman
said.

Bobby absorbed this information and blinked heavily. It
was not information he required.

'Look. Lads. I'm bone-tired and substantially cut. I just
want to get into my apartment that I pay the rent on and
am allowed into whenever I like and go to bed.'

'Sir,' the young man said, his face wholesomely indig-
nant. 'You don't understand. This is an emergency situation.
We came over to visit my Grand-aunt May and were
greeted with an *incredibly heavy* smell of what we are convinced is leaking gas in the second-storey hall. We went
from door to door to advise people to get out.'

'As instructed by the fire brigade,' the young woman
vouched.

'Ah, well,' Bobby said. 'I'm on the third floor anyway.'

'The whole building's potentially unsafe!' the young
woman said.

She was also in a denim shirt – pink to the young
man's baby blue – her expression as sincerely vexed as

his. They were dressed like an unironic country-and-western duo.

'Do you fuckers sing?' Bobby asked.

'W-what?' the young man responded.

Bobby seized on their confusion to insert his key in the lock and deftly open the door. He squeezed into the brief gap, then held the door fast behind him as the young man tried to pull it open.

'What the hell!' the girl shouted.

'I'm off to bed and nobody can stop me,' Bobby snarled. 'If the place goes up, tell them I went in willingly.'

There was indeed an *incredibly heavy* smell of what may well have been gas in the building, though to Bobby's cultivated faculties there was a faint but unmistakably herby back note to the atmosphere. Bobby suspected grass, a specialised or customised blend. But, then, he was drunk, his faculties impaired. Maybe it was gas, and not some ageing stoners toking obliviously away in their apartment. Bobby went carefully up the stairs. He tried to recall the things you were meant to do and not to do in order to avoid combusting. Ventilate space where possible, no naked flames, and be careful touching things lest friction prompt a catastrophic spark of static electricity. Something along those lines.

He unlocked his door and went into his apartment. He opened a window. He booted up his laptop, began preparing a joint with Becky's weed. He checked his mail. One of his oldest and most reliable clients, PussySlayer112, was back with a new request.

'Good old PussySlayer one-one-two,' Bobby muttered.

PussySlayer112 had gone to the effort of typing up the

commission as a Word doc, and when Bobby opened it he saw it was almost five thousand words long. He skim-read: elvish princesses from a video-game franchise Bobby was unfamiliar with, fisting, a dash of coprophagia, an extensive and almost clinically dry segue hypothesising how best to depict a dragon's hard-on. The usual. Bobby reminded himself, once again, that he needed to up his rates. The people who wanted this could only get it from him. He would start the job tonight, he decided, if he could just take the edge off his drunkenness with a bit of a smoke. He went over to the window. Out front of the building he could see the apparitions of his elderly neighbours, the blankets swaddling their hunched frames making them look like poorly pitched tents. The thought came to him, as it often did at night, that he was already dead, had been dead since the world began, just like everyone else, and that he was in heaven and that he was in hell, that heaven and hell were in the end the exact same place. He set the joint on his lip and brought the lighter to it. Friction: he looked out across the city sky and flicked the lighter's wheel, prepared for the night to go up all around him, but the night, as the night was wont to do, rolled massively and impersonally on. After a while, Bobby could hear the Dopplered gulling of the sirens as the fire engines made their approach.

# THE LOW, SHIMMERING
# BLACK DRONE

I WAS CROSSING the street with Caber's dogs, two big, pale-blond Labrador retriever half-brothers named Linus and Buddy, when I made a mistake. There was a coffee place across the road and in the coffee place's window there was an illuminated green sign that said OPEN but which, distracted by the dogs and with my head all muddled up on account of my father, I took to mean GO.

I stepped off the kerb and felt a car coming right for me. I turned to face it and the car braked, screeched, there was the awful sound of metal seizing precipitously up, I didn't move, I couldn't, but the car wasn't hitting me and it kept on not hitting me; after a moment I realised the car had come to a stop, its trembling grille close enough to reach out and touch.

Around my knees, Caber's dogs muscled and yowled, the leather of their leashes biting into the joints of my clenched fist.

The car's engine dropped to a steady growl, the growl of going nowhere. The windshield was an iridescent wash

of reflected city light. I could not make out the driver –
and even if I could all I would likely see would be a face in
a mask, as my face was in a mask – but I could sense the
mood burning off of them. Or I was thinking how I would
feel, and how, in that moment, I actually did feel: my heart
pounding with the furious relief of having avoided catas-
trophe by a hair's breadth, and looking around wild-eyed
for someone to blame. Only I was the one to blame, my
head all muddled up as I had stepped heedless and dreamy
off the kerb, pulling Caber's beloved dogs along with me.

The car continued to growl, stationary in the middle of
the street.

I eased my grip on the leashes and Linus and Buddy
barrelled across the road, dragging me after them.

The car moved off.

On the other side of the street, I could see that the coffee place was indeed open, albeit with the counter shunted
up into the doorway like a barricade, a single masked
employee inside, idly checking their phone in the empty,
gloomy interior.

There was no one else around, no other cars in the
street.

It was late May, the final days of a rainy, fog-strewn
spring, and though the harshest of the lockdown restrictions had eased, and people could leave their houses as
much as they wanted, the city still felt as becalmed and
tentative, as sullenly ghostly, as a new year's morning, all
the time.


What happened was my father had called. That's what had
my head all muddled up. Usually he rang blind drunk or

from the hospital. This time it was the hospital. He tended to ring after the first few days of sedation and anti-convulsion medicine had got him through the worst of the withdrawals and he was feeling not so bad, had been restored to a state of endurable badness.

My father lived out west, in Edmonton, Alberta. He came to Canada from Ireland eight years ago and found work in the oil fields out there. By the time I made my way to Toronto, three years back, he was out of that job. Out of any job. He had a one-bedroom apartment in downtown Edmonton, was living off some sort of pension or social security, and he was drinking. He had always drunk, of course, but once he lost the oil job he did nothing *but* drink. He drank all day, every day, and he would do this for months, until he reached exactly that point where he was sufficiently remorseful and afraid and sick enough to want to stop, but was also incapable of stopping. So what he did was ring the emergency services, make vague but plausible allusions to dying – to wanting or not wanting to die – appeals that in any case amounted to the same thing, and an ambulance would be dispatched to fetch him.

He did this at least a couple of times a year. The hospitalisations were a de facto detox, my father's aim to be admitted and looked after, unburdened of all capacity and agency, for as long as the hospital would agree to hold him. By the time they kicked him out he was sober. Each bout of sobriety would last around a month before he started drinking again and things began to go back to the way they were before; the way they were before, only each time a little worse.

*   *   *

Every morning for the last two months I walked Buddy
and Linus the four kilometres from Caber's place in Summerhill to Grange Park, a compact square of green located
downtown, next to the art gallery. Buddy and Linus were,
as I said, half-siblings. Same mother, different litters.
Buddy was the older of the two. He could not move so
well any more and once we got to the park he was content
to sit next to me and together we watched the diabolically
energetic Linus cavort out on the turf. There was hardly
anyone else about, so what I did was loop a long leash
around a tree trunk, feed Linus a hundred or so feet of
slack and lob a chew toy over and over on to the grass.
Within seconds the toy was back in my hand, sticky and
hot with a slaver that smelled almost smoky, Buddy jabbing the respiring black star of his nose into my face,
urging me to throw the toy again.

I was in Grange Park when I saw my father's number
flash up on the phone.

Nothing to worry about, my father told me when I picked
up, he'd been in a bad spot before he'd landed in the hospital but they'd knocked him out for much of the last few
days and while he was feeling weak he was also feeling
much, much better, and he was sleeping great. He told me
about the nurses, explaining how they continually checked
up on him and asked him how he was feeling, like I didn't
know what a nurse was. They were a marvel to him, this
little rotating cohort of people who, from his perspective,
behaved as if collectively possessed by some special affection for him. It didn't seem to matter to him that it was
their job, that he was their patient and that he could be

anybody. He loved the attention. He loved to complain about it.

'Here in my room every five minutes trying to get me to walk the hall on the walker but they won't listen when I say I don't have the strength for it,' he said.

'They want you up and about, I suppose,' I said. 'Are you eating?'

'What? Ah, no, I can't hold anything down, with the stomach pains on me. The diarrhoea, that's what I can't take,' he said, his voice brightening as he settled into one of his favourite topics, the ongoing degradation of his bowels. 'I don't mind the constipation. You take a pill and that gets sorted. It's the other stuff, this watery black scutter exploding down your leg if you don't make it to the toilet in two seconds. Which I can't, on account of the weakness in my legs. But the toilet is so far from the bed. It's their own fault then, isn't it, that them young ones have to come in and wipe my arse for me.'

'That's what they signed up for.'

'I've a thing now in a few days, a scan, a – whatyoucallit. What they think is there could be a blockage of some type, in my guts. That's what it feels like, this awful locked-up feeling in my guts.'

'They're the experts, but I reckon whatever's going on with your bowels has to do with the drink.'

'We'll see,' was all he said to that.

I asked him how things were in Edmonton, had the city been shut down like Toronto?

'Ah, I don't have a clue what's going on with all that. I don't go anywhere or see anyone anyway. This whole thing hasn't made a blind bit of difference to me.'

I told him I had to go and when I checked the log after, I saw that the call had lasted almost eight minutes, which was the typical duration of our exchanges, a duration to which I now instinctively kept. Eight minutes a call, weeks or months apart. Everything I needed to know about my father, I could find out in that time.

After my father's call, and after almost getting run over in the street, I made my way back to Caber's place with Linus and Buddy. All the houses in Caber's neighbourhood belonged to people with money, but Caber had one of those rich people's houses designed to elude attention. It was built on top of and down the leeside of a hill, so that from the street, all you could see was a set of monastically steep stone steps climbing to the entrance of a narrow black building overgrown with foliage and hardly bigger than the unwelcoming slab of the featureless front door set into it. It looked more like some sort of utility building than a home of any kind. But that was only the view permitted from the street. Once you climbed those steps and got inside the house, all was changed. The interior was vast and multilevelled, following the grade of the hill down which it was built in interlocking tiers, each room meticulously appointed and ultramodern. I had been living there, minding the dogs, ever since Caber fled north, and it still felt more like a hotel at which I was the only guest than anything resembling a home.

Nicholas Caber was a famous writer. By which I mean he was famous for a writer; every writer knew who he was and perhaps one in every two hundred civilians you mentioned his name to might recognise it, though they may not be sure from where. If they did not know his books, they tended to know at least one of the several movies made out of his books.

Caber wrote novels, stories, plays, screenplays. He'd been writing for decades. In interviews he had always credited his career to nothing more than 'my doglike indefatigability. When I write a bad book, I write another, and when I write a good book, I write another,' and by now he had ascended to that level of general renown where they stop giving you prizes and start giving you medals. Where an embassy might invite you for dinner twelve thousand kilometres away because the wife of the ambassador loved your last book.

When I first met Caber he had recently turned sixty and he was still very handsome. He was unmarried now but had been married three times, twice to the same woman. He had no children. He lived alone. He was tall and even in late middle age so thin he verged on gaunt, his suits hanging off him, as if his body had survived but never fully recovered from some formative ravaging, a child-hood wasting disease or blood disorder. His defining features were of course his eyes, in real life the pale, flecked, semi-translucent colour of dirty ice and which, in the black and white publicity photos his publishers insisted upon, appeared agelessly stark and phosphorescent, and seemed to look out and right through you, as an angel's might. That suggestion of celestial judgement – not a bad trait for a writer to have, or appear to have. We were, after all, living in a time when what people wanted from writers was judgement.

I got to know Caber by going to the readings and the talks, and after the readings and the talks, the bars. I had no money but in the bars I would buy a drink and make it last two drinks, staying on even as the crowd thinned out. I watched other people try to ingratiate themselves with him. Some came on deferential and some came on provocative, and he treated all with the same decorous evasiveness. I hung back, I said nothing, sustained by the obscure but persistent hope that if I stuck around long enough, I might eventually become interesting.

The night we became friends we were drinking with two other writers. Caber knew them. The two were a little younger and a lot less famous than Caber. They were performing for him, unleashing one decisive and sweeping opinion after another, about art and life and all the rest of it. Now and then one of them would turn to me, bug-eyed, teeth stained blue from the wine Caber was footing the bill for, and hiss 'And what do you think?' then swivel away from me before I could even attempt an answer. So far as they were concerned, I was a deadweight, struck dumb on the edge of the conversation, but Caber was not saying much either. He weathered the pair's endless pronouncing with a flat tolerant smile and in return offered only morsels of carefully innocuous industry gossip.

After they left, he asked me what I thought of them.

I told him I hadn't read their books. He said he didn't mean their books. He meant what did I think of *them*. I said nothing and this nothing, this merciful absence of human noise, pleased him. Caber fixed me with his eyes of bright, dirty ice.

'That's my problem,' he said. 'I'll put up with anybody.'

After that, he asked me what part of Ireland I came from – he had been there many times and loved the place – and I told him the sorry tale of how my father had ended up living out in Alberta, and Caber told me about Alberta, and the sorry tale of his father.

Like Charlie Furey, the teenage protagonist of his debut novel, *The World Exists for the First Time*, Caber grew up in a tiny rural Albertan town described, in that book, as a 'Canuck Hillbilly skidmark in the middle of the middle of nowhere'. Caber's father, like Charlie Furey's father, was a drunk who beat him up. In the novel the father deploys the end of a snapped-off antique chair leg recovered on one of his regular scavenging expeditions to the local junkyard. Quoting Charlie Furey: 'The chair leg looked sort of like a dog's leg, curved to a dainty little claw shape. Cabriole, I believe the style is called. It was made of a heavy, solid wood and left what looked like paw prints all up my back.'

My father drank all my life. The drinking, as drinking tends to do, got worse and worse, though he never laid a finger on us, physically. After he finally lost his job, and my mother finally kicked him out, he returned one morning, stinking of whiskey, to set the house on fire, though he did, to be fair, make sure neither of us was in it before striking the match. Then he skipped the country. We didn't hear anything from him, and could not be sure where he even was until word came back, through the whisper network of the diaspora, that he was in Edmonton, Alberta, in Canada. The radio silence continued on his part until I moved here. When word of my emigration made its way to him, presumably through that same whisper network, he did get in touch, sang all the right songs about his remorse, his regret and his misery. His plan, he told me, had been to burn the house down for the insurance, which would come through to my mother. She could then have used that payout to get herself a smaller place and live off the rest as a kind of supplementary pension. A lunatic scheme, if it was even true. In any case, the insurance company quickly deduced that the fire was not an accident and gave my mother nothing.

When the lockdown was first announced and nobody knew for sure how bad things were going to get, Caber did what many people with the means and opportunity did. He headed for the hills. He had a cottage in Muskoka. The night before he left he invited me over for dinner. I showed up at his door wearing a mask in public for the first time, and he laughed in my face. We ate shrimp and rice Caber had cooked himself, drank three bottles of wine out of his cellar. The authorities were already telling people not to travel unnecessarily, which Caber took to mean that if he did not leave right now he might end up stuck in the city indefinitely.

'I do think it's an irresponsible, hysterical and absolutely cowardly thing to do, and I sincerely hope that nobody else but me does it,' Caber said. 'But it can't be helped. I've a book to finish.'

'There's always a book,' I said.

'There's always a book,' Caber said.

We talked about it. The virus. The pandemic. Caber knew people on the city council, in the mayor's office. The city, anticipating scenarios where the health system might become overwhelmed, was quietly preparing contingencies, and contingencies for the contingencies. Talking about these things made my scalp prickle, like my skin was a piece of fabric being slowly knotted tighter and tighter at the base of my neck. Caber, by contrast, could see something like the funny side to it all, because he was getting to run away but also because even a world-stopping pandemic had brought with it a stroke of good fortune. He told me his phone had been going non-stop, even more than usual, because of a short, obscure novel he'd written almost ten years ago called *The Low, Shimmering Black Drone* which, with the onset of the pandemic, had lately returned to public attention.

The book begins with the unnamed protagonist, a writer, waking up in bed with his wife. As they go through their morning routine they hold a groggy, intimate conversation, in the way of any long-married couple, except the writer notices that every time his wife speaks, he hears, in the back of his head, a noise he describes as a 'low, shimmering black drone'. The same thing happens when the writer's daughter speaks to him, and later on, when he is out in public. Any human voice within earshot triggers the low, shimmering black drone. The writer describes the drone as just loud enough to make communication 'continually irritating and clumsy, but not so loud that communication is impossible'.

Soon other people begin to hear the low, shimmering black drone, and eventually everybody in the world. No explanation or source for the phenomenon can be determined by scientists or governments, and no solution, or even an effective mitigating measure, is ever found. Many people take vows of silence, revert to exclusively text-based communication, learn sign language. Authorities discourage gatherings that might include public speaking, but as the months and then years grind by with no end in sight, suicide rates, crime, violence and geopolitical instability surge. At first because of governmental pressure, and then of their own volition, people stop going out and interacting. Social life evaporates. The world begins to lose its mind.

There is the memorably unpleasant, if luridly unsubtle, scene at the climax of the book when the writer, stranded in his soundproofed apartment (his wife and daughter are long gone) and half-mad with loneliness, savages his ear-drums with a fountain pen in an attempt to save himself from ever again being subjected to the drone. The book ends months later, with the healing, newly deaf writer restored to a kind of peace, isolated but productive, work-ing on a new book:

*He sat at his table and wrote on through the night, turn-ing out one sentence and then another, and another and another. It had been a long time since the sentences had come like this. He did not feel tired. He felt only the cold and lucid ecstasy of the flow, the sentences coming and coming. By the time the morning light was creeping across the table, he was done. He looked up. Branches were mov-ing in the breeze outside his apartment window. He watched a leaf detach, flashing silver as it turned and turned in the air and dropped from sight. Already the feel-ing of cold and lucid ecstasy was emptying out of him, fading like it had never existed. He knew why. Out of the still depths of his self-inflicted silence he heard it rising towards him again, the low, shimmering black drone.*

The reviews at the time were tepid and puzzled, most critics interpreting the novel as an overheated and self-indulgent allegory about the struggle of a sensitive artist to acclimatize themselves to the clamour and distraction of the modern world, and asking, quite reasonably, why anyone who was not a writer would give a shit about such a predicament. And no one did: the book found neither acclaim nor an audience and faded quickly from the cultural conversation.

But this year, within weeks of the first wave of lockdowns, an *NYRB* piece by James Wood articulated the critic's eerie experience of reading the book just as New York shut down around him. That same weekend the actress Emily Ratajkowski lauded the book on Instagram. Articles and social media mentions proliferated and soon *The Low, Shimmering Black Drone* made a belated debut on the bestseller list. In short order a streaming service announced they had bought the rights to the novel and were fast-tracking it into a mini-series. Now journalists were ringing and emailing Caber day and night to ask him how he had come to write this uncannily prescient fable about a society struck by a catastrophic exogenous event that renders unmediated social intercourse so interpersonally hazardous that eventually everyone ends up sealed inside their homes, alone and increasingly deranged.

'Basically I just liked the phrase "the low, shimmering black drone",' he told me. 'It appealed to my weakness for excessively poetic titles.'

We were in the sitting room, drinking cognac. Buddy was up on the sofa tucked right in beside Caber, Caber stroking his fur. Even the excitable Linus was down on all fours on the rug in front of the switched-off fireplace, watching something indiscernible through the enormous windows overlooking Caber's floodlit back garden, which to me seemed only empty and still.

'From that I spun out this flimsy, clumsy piece of sub-Saramago-ian bullshit that none of my editors really liked, and actually *I* didn't even like, but it was done and I needed the money. So we put it out, it dropped off the face of the earth and once the wound of its vanishing reception crusted over I never thought about it again.'

'What's it feel like to be a prophet?' I asked him one drink on.

'I want you to know I have emphatically refuted any charges of prophecy, prescience or perspicuity. Good Lord. Imagine claiming someone was a prophet just because they said "in the future things are going to get worse".'

'Anyway,' he continued, 'the reason I wanted you over wasn't just to say goodbye. I need a favour. I was thinking you could stay here. Until I get back.'

He nodded at Linus and patted Buddy's haunch.

'I can't bring these guys with me. I need someone here with them. I need them walked every day. I'll pay you. Six hundred dollars a week. You can eat me out of house and home, drink as much wine as you like. Groceries are delivered every Sunday, the cleaner comes every Friday. Stay here, write here, do what you like. I don't think you'll want for anything.'

I lived downtown, in the basement level of a house. The three storeys above my head accommodated an indeterminate number of lead-footed university students. I pretended to think about Caber's offer. When I didn't answer straight away he said, 'I know this is obnoxious of me.'

'It's fine,' I said, trying to sound casual. 'I can do it. You don't need to pay me anything.'

'OK,' he said, offering his hand to shake on the deal. When I took it, he said, 'Seven hundred a week. I won't take no for an answer.'

Back in the early sixties, my paternal grandfather, a man named Ivor Mullen from Crossmolina in Mayo Ireland, came here to work for the Canadian Pacific Railway company. He travelled all around the country, but it was in Alberta, of all places, that he met Brigit Cain, a seamstress from Gort. There, Brigit Mullen gave birth to my father. They returned to Ireland when he was still a baby. Perhaps it made a kind of sense, all those years later, for my father to flee to Edmonton after he burned our house down. Nobody runs away, so much as back.

I inherited Canadian citizenship through my father, which was how I was able to follow him over three years ago. My reactivated citizenship meant I could stay in Canada as long as I wanted, leave when I wanted, and so, emboldened by the prospect that failure was always an option, I bought a one-way ticket to Toronto. Toronto was as close as I intended to get to him. I had no interest in confronting my father or intervening in any way in his life. My only goal, once I got here, was to finish writing my book. I had been writing it for years before I came to

Toronto and, years later, I was still writing it. For money I got by on bits and pieces: sold cell phones in a mall kiosk, delivered takeout, did a stint as an elementary school crossing guard. I applied for grants and sometimes I got them. All the time I kept writing.

The problem was that I did not want to write a book about my father. Elimination of the father as subject was the single compositional rule I had imposed upon myself. But because the book was not about him, it had ended up threatening to become about everything else. At various points the book resembled a dirty-realist *Bildungsroman* about an inexplicably fatherless young man in small-town Ireland, a picaresque historical romance about an Irish expat working on the North American railroads in the middle of the twentieth century, a splenetic Bernhard-style monologue about a malevolent cipher travelling around a fictional country burning down houses ... I had written several books and no book and was still writing the book; I had written a thousand or so pages around an absented centre I did not want to acknowledge or approach.

Caber, of course, told me to stop fucking around and just write about my father.

'Everyone's already written about their fathers,' I told him with exasperation. '*You've* written about your father. It's done, it's done a million times over. No one wants to read that shit any more.'

'There's a million books about fathers, sure,' Caber conceded. 'So what's one more?'

A few days after the call from the hospital my father rang again. I was on the patio in Caber's back garden, dishing out food for the dogs. The garden was at the bottom of the hill, the house above it a floating elaboration of concrete, stone and glass descending like a river arrested magically in place.

'Tonight's the night,' my father told me, meaning the colonoscopy. 'They're going to stick a camera up there and see what they can see.'

'Lovely,' I said, scraping out the last of a 25-dollar tub of grass-fed beef into the dog bowls.

'I *know* it's a tumour, I can feel it,' he said, sounding almost excited.

Last year my father told me he was forgetting things. He told me he kept getting confused about what day it was, and more and more found himself standing in the supermarket aisle with no idea what he was looking for. One of his brothers had had Alzheimer's and my father told me he was worried he might have it too. I told him to go to his doctor, that there were tests he could take if he was worried. I have no idea if he did so. At a certain point he simply stopped bringing up the memory thing.

Another time he rang from the hospital, not in withdrawal, but with some kind of small fracture in a bone in his back. I asked if he had fallen while drunk, sure that he had, but he wouldn't admit it. He kept speculating about osteoporosis and then, as abruptly as the Alzheimer's, never mentioned it again.

My father wanted what every alcoholic who cannot quit wants: exoneration. To die of something other than drink would, by his sodden logic, exonerate him. Could you have been that chronic an alcoholic if you didn't even die of it?

'They putting you under?' I asked.

'All the way. Have you ever been under? It's the funniest feeling. They hook the needle into your arm and tell you count backwards from ten, and you think sure, no problem. By seven your head starts swimming and before you know it you're gone. You wake up feeling like you've slept for a thousand years. It's bliss.'

We must have been about eight minutes into the call because I felt a familiar tightness gathering in my jaw. Buddy and Linus were pacing nearby, disciplined enough to wait for my signal before they attacked their respective bowls. They were watching me with their mouths agog and dripping, like I was the meal.

'Good luck with your arsehole,' I told my father. 'I have to go.'

Caber rang most weekends because weekends in the cottage were crushingly boring, he admitted, once you had enough of the view. He would make me put the dogs on. He talked to them and they crooned to the sound of his voice.

'You're making them crazy,' I told him.

'There's a little torturer inside all of us,' he said. 'Listen to this.' The line was faint, compressed. Caber's voice sounded as if it was being squeezed through a long, tight tube. He really was in the middle of nowhere. 'This is me writing a friend in Manhattan this morning: "I see it reported that the case numbers are plateauing down there and that things are beginning to stabilise, good news for you." God Almighty. Did you ever think we would end up here, exchanging such evocative sci-fi prose?'

'I want to ask how the writing's going,' I said.

'Now, now. Do that and I'll have to ask you.'

'You said that's why you're up there.'

Caber sighed, or affected to.

'You think after – what, thirteen books? – I'd know what I was doing. But this one is just like all the others. I'll get there. I always do. But for now, it's just debris I'm crawling around in.'

'Debris?' I said.

'Yeah,' he said.

'Now that feeling, I know,' I said.

June arrived. I was sitting at one of Caber's desks just inside the double doors that opened out on to the garden patio. I was back in the debris – writing. Buddy was warming himself on the flagstones. Linus was tacking back and forth at the bottom of the garden, alertly following the movement of birds or squirrels in the trees on the other side of the fence.

My phone rang. A number I didn't know, but I knew the area code. Alberta. I picked up.

'Is that Mr Mullen?'

'Mr Mullen is my father,' I said lamely, the old joke.

'I'm looking for Sean. Sean Mullen.'

'I'm him.'

'Your father is actually why I'm calling, Sean. I'm Dr Sparling, one of the doctors here at Grey Nuns Hospital in Edmonton. Your father asked me to ring you, to update you on the results of his recent colonoscopy. We weren't anticipating it, but uh, we did in fact find something and your father wanted me to talk to you about that?'

'"Something",' I quoted.

Polyps, Sparling said, a cluster of large and serrated polyps. *Large* did not sound good. *Serrated* did not sound good. Sparling said she had removed what she could during the colonoscopy and biopsied the extracted material. The results had come back confirming that my father's bowels were either cancerous or precancerous. I did not quite catch the distinction, distracted as I was by Linus, who had become suddenly interested in a certain spot along the base of the fence. I watched the animal lower his head and commence frenetically digging, clods of dirt spitting up into the air either side of him. Sparling said that my father was going straight back in for surgery tomorrow morning. The dirt continued to fly and, with a slithering, eel-like contraction, Linus squeezed his head, shoulders and the front half of his torso down and into the gap he had created. His rear legs trembled, braced, and with a second and final shove the back half of his torso followed the first and the dog was gone.

'What the fuck,' I said.

'I know this is difficult information to receive,' Sparling said.

'OK. I just. My father knows about this?' I said. 'Why didn't he call me?'

'He's, uh, resting right now. And he wanted me to call,' Sparling said. 'In a difficult circumstance like this, sometimes a patient prefers a doctor to speak to a loved one first, in order to give a clearer picture of things and answer any questions that the loved one might have.'

'Me being the loved one,' I said.

'Of course.'

I went outside and Buddy got up and followed me to the end of the garden. I looked down at the ragged chute of soil beneath the fence that Linus had improvised and wedged himself through. The fence itself was tall, taller than me. I placed an eye up to the sliver of space between adjacent slats. I couldn't see much – foliage, rocks, shadow.

'Your father is at the beginning of a difficult journey,' Sparling said.

'His whole life's been a difficult journey,' I said.

Silence. I heard the doctor clear her throat.

'OK. Well. That's the situation as it stands now, Mr Mullen. If you have any questions—'

'I won't,' I said and hung up.

I began bellowing Linus's name over the fence. I had no idea if he was just on the other side, foraging a few feet from me, or racing at thirty kilometres an hour in the direction of Newfoundland. I went back inside, leashed Buddy up, put on a mask and circled the neighbourhood for an hour, ringing doorbells and traversing the brushy alleys between and behind the properties. I checked the house, in case Linus had returned, then decided to leave Summerhill and go downtown to Grange Park, good old Buddy limping diligently along with me, on the off-chance that Linus had headed that way.

In the last few days restrictions had eased again. People were permitted back inside stores and cafes, though in limited numbers. As we arrived downtown, I began to see them, the staggered lines of people queuing outside department stores. And there seemed to be more vehicles in the street after months of nothing but police cruisers and ambulances.

It was a beautiful evening in the city, the setting sun streaking the blue sky rose-gold. A small crowd had gathered in Grange Park. Groups of young people, families. There were people sunbathing and lounging on picnic blankets, drinking wine from coolers and eating takeout out of Styrofoam boxes, kids playing peekaboo among the enormous bonelike curves of the park's bronze Henry Moore sculpture, *Large Two Forms*. There was a man and a woman in Lycra and taped fists throwing practice punches at each other. The crowd consisted of, at most, forty people, some masked, some not, but after the nervous emptiness of the past few months, it seemed as if a festival had broken out. I sat down with Buddy, in our usual spot, from where we would watch Linus tear across the grass.

I looked up my father's number. Still not saved in my phone as a name, just a logged row of digits I only half knew by heart. Since we'd started talking again, my father had always been the one to initiate contact; fair enough, I had always thought, because I was the injured party, I was the one to whom redress was owed.

I dialled his number. Ring, ring, ring. It went to voicemail. He had botched his personalised message – all I heard was a surprised, split-second snatch of indrawn breath dilating in exasperation before the cut to the beep.

'It's me,' I said. 'I talked to your doctor. She gave me the news. She said you're going into surgery first thing tomorrow. I probably won't get to talk to you until after, now. Anyway. I just thought I'd try you.'

I paused, waited a moment, and then I said, 'Maybe you were right after all.'

I hung up and watched the man and the woman boxing. The woman was masked, and what was visible of her face looked flushed, strands of hair sticking to her gleaming forehead. The man was wearing a fitted glove with an outsize palm, sort of like a baseball mitt, that the woman was hurling punches into.

There was the little flat *pfft* of each hit, followed by the larger *PAP* of the hit's echo.

'See,' I heard the man say. 'It's that sound when it connects right. That sound never lies.'

I rang Caber. He picked up and I explained what had happened, how I had taken a call – though I refrained from telling him who the call was from or what it was about – and how Linus, in the space of what seemed like a few seconds, had dug a hole out of nothing at the end of the garden and escaped.

Caber listened, he let me speak, then he let out a low, measured sigh.

'How long has he been missing?'

'It's been . . . almost two hours now,' I said. 'I've been looking for him the whole time.'

'Two hours? Why didn't you call me sooner?'

'I know. I should have.'

Caber did not speak immediately. His silences were tormentingly complete. You could read any terrible thing into them. I was glad I could not see his eyes, their palely burning regard like another order of silence.

'I asked you to do one thing, Sean,' he said, with wounding mildness.

'I'll keep looking.'

'I'll start packing,' he said. 'I can get back to the city by tonight.'

'I'm sorry.'

'You just . . . watched him dig a hole and run for it?'

The woman threw a hook that connected with particular meatiness, the crack of that hit reviving a dormant instinct in Buddy. He swerved his head and growled in the direction of the boxers. I stroked the suede-soft flesh of his ear until he settled again. Apart from his missing sibling, I believed it was the crowd – the sudden, restored presence of all these people – that was disconcerting him.

'It happened so quick,' I told Caber. 'I just didn't think he'd bolt for it like that.'

'That's the thing about dogs, Sean,' Caber said. The line was as bad as ever, his voice thin and remote in my ear, blistered with static, barely there. 'You can domesticate them all you like, you can turn them into the most loyal and obedient creatures on earth, but all it takes is you not paying attention for one second, just *one* second, and *whssht* – like that, they're gone.'

# THE 10

## 1

Danny Faulkner felt a tingle in his scalp, jolted upright in his seat and smacked instinctively at the spot on his head. He blinked, examined his blank palm and looked around the room, faintly irate, as if it was someone else that had struck him, then sat still and held his breath until he could see it, the dark vibrating dot of a midge tracing a wavering circle in the air.

Danny yawned and shifted in his seat. He had fallen asleep, right there at his desk. The laptop's screensaver had come on. The screensaver image was a landscape, depicting a valley of densely clustered, rounded, node-like rocks covered in a delicate layer of palely glowing green moss. The photo was other-worldly, like the surface of an alien planet, but it was only a lava field in Iceland, according to the caption.

The midge circled buzzing in the air and drifted in front of the window, where Danny lost it in the light. Out on the lot the sun was beating relentlessly down on the still and silent rows of cars. The sky had no clouds in it and was the bright chemical blue of the dye they put in ice pops. Just looking at the sky was making Danny thirsty. It was a gorgeous Friday afternoon in July, but what the weather was doing was none of Danny's business, confined as he was to the dim and sweltering back office of his father's Nissan dealership until the clock struck five.

Danny looked up at the grilled vents in the ceiling. He reckoned there was something wrong with the room's air conditioning. Air seemed to be circulating, it just wasn't *doing* anything. Danny decided to test his suspicion. He snapped shut the laptop, rolled his chair into the middle of the room, and carefully – recklessly but carefully – stepped up on to the seat and reached for one of the ceiling vents. He was right; the jet of air dropping from the vent was no cooler than the tepid air already in the room. The midge zipped by his ear. He spouted his lips and blew futilely in the bug's direction. The chair began quaking skittishly on its casters. Danny steadied himself and jumped to the floor as the chair shot out from under him and thudded into the wall.

A few moments later Danny's father, JJ, stuck his head into the office.

'What was that?' he said.

'What was what?'

'Don't be buckassing.'

'I'm not buckassing,' Danny said, glancing at that section of wall the chair had collided with. He thought he saw a faint grey scuff-mark, looked quickly back at his father.

'Here,' he said, 'what's with the air con? It's like a furnace in here.'

'It's sticky, all right,' JJ said. 'I'll get Grealy on it. Did you hear from Ben?'

Ben was Danny's older brother. He lived in Dublin. Danny shook his head.

'He's down tonight on the train. Only I've to meet that bandit of an accountant Morrison this evening and I can't get out of it. Would you be OK to pick him up?'

'I was going to head to Shauna's,' Danny said. Shauna Vaughan was Danny's girlfriend.

'So that's a no?' JJ sighed.

'No, I can,' Danny relented. 'I can get him, no bother.'

'Good man,' JJ said. As they talked, JJ unbuttoned the cuff of his left shirtsleeve, rolled it up and commenced rubbing methodically at his forearm. Danny saw what he always saw when his father did this: the glossy, serpentine streak of pale scar tissue that ran from JJ's wrist almost up to his elbow. Danny's father had been in a car crash years ago, back when he was not much older than Danny, and his left arm had been smashed to pieces. Danny had seen the pictures from that time; an implausibly younger JJ lying in a hospital bed with a look of sheepish forbearance on his face, the arm suspended above him on a rig. In another picture, JJ drinking a beer in their living room, sitting on a garish orange and brown sofa Danny did not remember in an Italia 90 jersey, aiming a defiant thumbs-up to the camera, a device called a fixator attached to his arm. The fixator resembled miniature scaffolding, an arrangement of rods and pins sunk into the skin of his arm and which he had worn for months until his bones had knitted back together. JJ still suffered regular spells of pain in the arm, as well as his back and neck. Danny was eighteen now and had been only three months old at the time of the crash. He and his mother Helen had not been in the car, but Ben had.

'Be good to see him,' Danny said.

'Has he not been down since you got back?' JJ asked.

'He has not.'

'I've a picture in my head, clear as day, of the four of us sat having dinner together, like a month ago.'

'I can assure you that did not happen.'

'I'll take your word for it,' JJ said, letting go of his arm and sighing with satisfaction. 'You'll be at Shauna's for the night, I suppose?'

'Probably.'

'Are you heading into town?'

'Whatever Shauna wants.'

'It's Friday night. Will that young one not want to be out dancing?'

'Shauna likes a dance. It's not my thing.'

'You don't go dancing with her?'

'She dances with her mates.'

'Ah, lad,' JJ sighed.

'Shauna doesn't mind if I don't dance.'

'And how do you know she doesn't?' JJ asked, but before Danny could answer he said, 'Love will have its way with you in the end, buck. Tell her little bollocks of a father I said hello.'

'Will do.'

'Ben's train,' JJ said as he stepped from the room. 'Six forty-five. Good man.'

The rest of the day crawled. Danny could not wait to tear out the door and race across town to the Vaughans' house.

And yet, when five o'clock finally arrived, Danny found himself dawdling, rendered pleasurably irresolute by the imminency of his freedom. He packed away the laptop and tidied the desk, drifted around the room releasing the cords of the window blinds, watching each blind skitter upward with a frantic shuttering sound. He licked his thumb, rubbed ineffectually at the smudge on the wall where the chair had hit it. He sat up on the table and scrolled through his phone.

He checked Ben's number. Their last exchange was a week ago, Ben responding with a single crylaughing face to some stupid meme Danny had forwarded him. Danny texted *will pick you up tonight.*

Danny went to Shauna's number and realised Shauna had sent him a message just before noon:

*Hey hun let me know how yr day is going x x.*

Danny had not replied. As long and dull as the day had been, he had somehow not been able to stir himself for the five seconds it would have taken to text her back. He wasn't sure why, except that tedium was its own kind of discouragement, that sitting at a desk not doing one thing somehow made you less inclined to do another, even if you wanted to.

*Sorry day was grand busy leaving now x* he texted.

Outside, Danny opened the door of his car and left it open to air the vehicle out. He leaned against the boot, pinched the damp scratchy fabric of his shirt from his chest, and looked out across the lot. The lot was surrounded by a shabby scrawl of chain-link fencing the father should have long ago ripped out and replaced. It glimmered in spots and in other spots was black where the silver paint had flaked off the links. Beyond the fence a weedy interval of waste ground led up to a pair of train tracks. Ballina station was a quarter mile west of the dealership. Three times a day a stoic little two-carriage train set out from Ballina for Manulla Junction and three times a day it came back. Manulla Junction was where the central line from Dublin connected to Ballina. Ben would be getting off at Manulla within the hour and would be in Ballina twenty minutes after that.

A message came in on Danny's phone. He figured it was Shauna or Ben getting back to him, but it wasn't.

*Chancing the arm again. Training this Sunday @ 1pm*
*You do know the boys want u back*
  *B*

'You do know the boys want u back.'

Danny had to smile at that. B was Budgie McAllister, one of Danny's old youth coaches, now Ballina Town FC's senior team coach, and ever since Danny had returned to Ballina the man had been only dying to get Danny into the fold. Half the lads on the team had been in touch, most no doubt at Budgie's behest, begging Danny to come back and play.

All through his childhood, Danny Faulkner had been the best footballer on any pitch, at any level he played at. That wasn't something Danny was big-headed or boastful about, it was just a sentiment that had been expressed to him so many times, by so many people, that he could only accept it as true, a fact as prosaically self-evident as the fact that he was five ten and had green eyes. By the time he was eight there were scouts flying in from England to watch him play and when he was nine he was offered a trial at Manchester United's academy. He was invited back regularly over the following years. He would travel with one of his parents, usually JJ, stay a few weeks and come home. When he turned sixteen he made the decision to move to Manchester and attend the academy full-time. The club placed him with a family, sorted him with tutors for schooling, but it wasn't long after he moved over that things began to go wrong; not wrong exactly, it was just that certain of Danny's peers began to progress beyond him, physically, technically and even in their mentality, at a pace he could not match.

He did what he could to catch up. He stayed behind after training, booked double gym sessions, counted every last calorie that went into his body. At night, in the lonely bedroom of his Manchester digs, he listened to mindset audiobooks and studied academy-supplied video footage of his performances with prosecutorial dispassion, hunting only for the weak points and flaws in his game. But the gap between him and the other lads continued to grow. The coaches could see it. Danny had always played as the 10, the playmaker and attacking focus of the team, but they started moving him into other positions in order to, as they put it, 'expand his game'. They tried him on the wing, but he wasn't quick enough; up front, but he wasn't big enough; at the back, but he did not have the defensive discipline.

Danny endured a good eighteen months of this piecemeal dismantlement of his footballing identity. His game became cautious, inexpressive, functional. At a certain point, he could tell management were no longer even watching him, not really. They had ended their concern in him and were only keeping him around because you needed raw numbers, you needed bodies of a sufficient standard out there on the pitch so that the handful of lads who *were* going to make it could keep developing. And that's what Danny had become; a living training cone, one of those hundreds of panting, lead-footed boys he had run rings around, with the happy, cold-blooded guilelessness of the prodigy, all through his childhood.

Early April, as the end of the academy season loomed, the coaches scheduled Danny in for a meeting. JJ caught a last-minute flight over and was in the room when the assistant youth coach informed Danny that the club was not going to offer him a senior contract. The coach tried to give Danny the placating spiel they must give every lad they cut loose. Danny stopped the man short, told him it was fine, that he'd known it was coming.

JJ at least did not make things worse by losing it on Danny's behalf, just sat in his chair clenching his jaw and listening. After, out in the hall, he hugged Danny and growled, 'Fuck them, we'll show them.' By which his father meant there were other options. And that was true. Even now that was true. It was not too late for Danny to make himself available for trials. He had contacts in the UK, he still had a reputation among scouts. A career in the game was salvageable, albeit likely at a much lower level. If he wanted it badly enough he might find a way back in, but the heart had gone out of it for him. The day he was cut loose by United was the day Danny decided he was done with football, and he was still done with it, because it was an awful thing, maybe the worst thing, to discover that in the end you were only good enough to get far enough to find out that you were not good enough. So he packed up, came home and spent a long time lying on his childhood bed staring at the cruel, arrogant visage of Cristiano Ronaldo tacked to the back of the bedroom door. His parents weren't sure what to do. He insisted he was not going back to England. His education had been a mishmash of the Irish and English systems; his parents said they wanted him to go back to Muredach's, the boys' secondary school, and sit his final-year exams. But Danny's peers – Shauna included – were off to college in a couple of months. The idea of doing a year on his own, back in a school he'd not set foot in in almost three years, was like something from an anxiety dream. The parents kept at him and he kept saying no. Eventually JJ told him – didn't ask him – told him, that Danny was going to come work for him, for as long as it took for him to decide what he was going to do, and so that's what happened. His daddy bailed him out. He'd been in the dealership since.

What Danny wanted to do now was text Budgie back: *FUUUUUUUUUUUCKOOOOOOOOOOOOFF.* Instead, he put away his phone and climbed into his car.

## 2

Danny's Friday-evening routine was always the same. Come five o'clock, if he wasn't working late, he would lace it directly across town to Shauna's folks' place. Sometimes they just hung out, ate pizza and watched films. Mostly they went out with Shauna's friends. Danny didn't mind either way. He was content to do whatever Shauna wanted to do.

The Vaughans ran a bed and breakfast out of their big house on the other side of Ballina town. When Danny pulled into the pebbled drive, he saw the father's car, and the older sister's, but not Shauna's or the mother's. No guest vehicles either. A set of broad steps lined with potted plants led up to the front door of the house but Danny, as was custom, made his way around the side of the property, unhooked the iron eye-latch of the gate, cut into a raw-planked wooden fence, and followed a flagstone path into the back garden. The rear door of the house was framed by a pretty profusion of climbing ivy and cosily concealed as a magical door in a kids' movie. Danny knocked.

'The man himself,' Matty Vaughan said, opening the door and standing back to let Danny enter the long, low-ceilinged kitchen. Matty had an apron tied around him and was wielding a pair of tongs. The room was humid with cooking. Evie, Shauna's older sister, was sitting on a stool by the counter, her two-year-old daughter Beth Anne up on her lap.

'Well, Evie,' Danny said.

'Well,' Evie muttered without looking up. She was propping Beth Anne on her knees, clutching the child's midriff while attempting to one-handedly write some-thing down on the bright yellow square of a Post-it note that was sliding around on the counter under the pressure of her pencil.

'How's tricks, Danny?' Matty said, his face bright red from the heat, wrinkles of sweat on his temple.

'Can't complain,' Danny said. 'How's business?'

Matty wiped his forehead with the back of his arm.

'Ah, not a peep tonight, though we do have a couple of bookings pencilled in for tomorrow. You're straight from work, by the looks of things?'

'I am.'

'How's JJ?'

'The same as ever. He said to say hello.'

'I bet he did,' Matty said with a smile. Every week Matty put Danny through a version of this same conversation, and every week Danny submitted a version of the same answers. Matty Vaughan used to teach maths and chemistry in Muredach's. He had taught Danny until Danny left for England, and before that had taught Danny's father and all Danny's uncles. Since his retirement from teaching, Matty and his wife Marie had run the B&B full-time. Though they were the kind of family that seemed well off, Danny figured they must have required, or at least welcomed, the income, for he could think of few things more disquieting than permitting a regular stream of strangers to traipse in and out of what was meant to be your house, even if it was a house as big as this one.

'Shauna in?' Danny asked.

'Have you seen Shauna, Evie?' Matty asked.

Evie looked at Danny. With a shock that was almost illicit, Danny saw a dark stain gleaming inside her mouth. It looked like blood, an injury. Evie bared her teeth and spat something precisely out. She noticed Danny looking.

'I'm after biting the top off that fucking pencil,' she said.

'Why on earth are you eating a pencil?' Matty said.

'Only I saw Shauna's car isn't out there,' Danny said.

'Then I guess she's gone,' Evie said, dabbing her lip and tasting her finger. To her father she said, 'I'm going to do the shop tomorrow. I'm getting the list down now so I won't forget anything when I'm wandering through Dunnes hungover at ten in the morning.'

'That's very organised of you,' Matty said.

Danny noticed now that little Beth Anne was in one of those onesie pyjama suits, while Evie was done up to go out, make-up and tan, skinny white jeans and heels. Evie lived a little outside of Ballina, in the parish of Corroy. So she had dropped over to leave Beth Anne with the grand-parents for the night.

'Mind yourselves now, everybody,' Matty said, tugging an oven glove on to his hand. He opened the oven and transferred with a resonant metal clonk a pan laden with a joint of furiously sizzling roast beef on to the stove top.

'Smells unreal,' Danny said.

'You're welcome to join us.'

'I'll – I'll see what Shauna wants to do.'

'Actually I believe it was Marie took Shauna's car this afternoon.'

'Why did Mammy take Shauna's car?' Evie asked.

'Because Mammy's car is in the shop,' Matty said.

'What's wrong with it?'

'The mysteries of combustion I leave to the experts,' Matty said, nicking a sliver of meat off the joint and tast-ing it. 'That's the stuff.'

Beth Anne, docile on her mother's lap, was playing with a book. It was a book for babbies; the pages weren't made of paper but thick solid plastic, and the gimmick with the book

was that it played recordings of nursery rhymes as you
turned the pages. Beth Anne was slapping and pawing at it,
disinterestedly clattering the hard pages back and forth, so
that each burst of song was interrupted by the next.

*Baa baa bla—Hickory dick—Row row row Twinkle twink—*
Matty and Evie seemed immune to the noise.

'You'd think she was doing it on purpose,' Danny said.

'To antagonise you,' Evie said. 'And sure maybe she is.'

Danny smiled uneasily. Evie's presence always made him a
little uncomfortable. She was thirty-two or so, not that old
really, and she was a widow. Scott Kinsella had been the name
of Beth Anne's father. Kinsella had passed away only weeks
after Beth Anne was born. Danny could not claim to have
known the lad well, but he had met him a few times. Kinsella
had worked as a field engineer for the phone company. The
only exchange with Kinsella Danny can even remember was
at somebody's wedding. Ben was there, catastrophically
drunk, and he kept asking Kinsella, 'Do you go up the poles?
Scotty, do you go up the poles?' until Kinsella, with a tolerant
smile, had said, 'Yeah, I go up the poles.'

Kinsella died of a brain haemorrhage, doing nothing
more strenuous than sitting at home with Evie and the
baby of an evening, watching the telly. He got a bad headache and then he passed out and, though an ambulance
rushed him to hospital, that was that. Kinsella's death was
so viciously sudden it sometimes felt to Danny like it hadn't
happened at all. Even now, whenever Danny had cause to
remember Scott Kinsella, he was struck by the odd but
persistent notion that he had somehow misapprehended
the whole event, that it was in fact some other poor lad he
was half-acquainted with who had dropped dead out of the

blue and who Danny had somehow got mixed up with Scott Kinsella. Which was all to say that if Kinsella were to amble into the Vaughans' kitchen right this moment, with an oblivious half-smile on his lips and nothing to say to Danny but 'long time, no see', Danny would, he felt, not be surprised.

'Is Shauna off with Mammy, then?' Evie suggested to Matty.

'She's not. Mammy went to visit Auntie Tracy in Castlebar,' Matty said, lifting the lid on a pot and inspecting the spuds wobbling away in the boiling water. 'So we have another mystery on our hands. Where on earth is my youngest daughter, Shauna?'

'I can give her a shout,' Danny said.

'That might be an idea, Danny,' Matty said.

Danny dialled her up and let himself into the back garden as it rang out.

'Well, hon. I'm standing in your back garden, wondering where you are. So's your oul buck. I thought you'd be here. Give me a shout when you can,' Danny told her voicemail.

Probably, she was at Alice's. Alice Lyons was Shauna's best mate. The Lyonses' place was a twenty-minute walk a little north of here, in Belleek Woods estate.

'I left her a message,' Danny told Matty and Evie when he went back inside. 'I don't know. I guess I'll head off.'

Matty pointed to a plate of sliced beef on the kitchen island.

'That's for you, young fella. Get it into you.'

'Thanks so much,' Danny said. He was hungry. The beef was lovely. He tried not to hoover it in one go.

'I'm sure herself will turn up any minute now,' Matty said.

'I actually have to go collect Ben from the train,' Danny said. 'It's due in shortly.'

'Ben is down. Oh, lovely,' Matty said. 'How's he faring up there in Dublin?'

'All good, as far as I know. I haven't actually seen him since I got back.'

'He must be busy, no more than yourself. It's nice when you can corral everyone back under the one roof. It gets harder to do as time goes on.'

Evie had her phone out and was staring into it. She looked up and said, 'Danny, if you're off, would you mind running me into town?'

'Sure,' he said.

'So no one is going to stay here now and eat this beautiful dinner with me?' Matty asked.

'Won't Mam be back?' Evie said, clutching Beth Anne against her midriff as she came up off the stool.

'I have no idea,' Matty said.

'Well, you have herself here to keep you company. Cut that meat up fine enough and she might even eat a bit of it for you. Goodbye now, pickle,' Evie said, kissing Beth Anne's crown and passing her into Matty's arms. Evie snatched up the Post-it of grocery items and stuck it to her father's forehead. Danny stood aside to let Evie out the back door while Matty peeled the sticker from his forehead and looked at Danny with a lingering, almost apologetic, expression.

'Mind yourself, Danny,' he said.

\*    \*    \*

Evie was meeting friends at Harrison's pub so that's where Danny was taking her. Now that they were in his car, alone together, he wasn't sure what to say. Danny did not know Evie well, and on top of that there was the issue of her widowhood. She had not been married to Kinsella, so technically that might not be the term, but in Danny's head that's what she was. This condition of widowhood meant the usual questions you could trot out in the guise of small talk – *What's going on? How you been?* – seemed somehow callous. Even though it had been a couple of years since Kinsella's passing, Danny did not want to seem blithe, or unnecessarily stir up a delicate feeling in Evie. But then neither did he want to treat her like there was radiation coming off her. So he was stuck sitting there, looking straight out the windshield, feigning total concentration on the road. He could feel Evie looking at him, the gathering tension of her regard as the silence ticked by like seconds. Probably thinking, what's up with this fella? Then she spoke.

'You still don't drink, do you, Danny?'

'Drink? No.'

'I always forget that about you, and then I remember. And you're still sticking to that now that you're – now that you're back home?'

*Now that you're not going to make it as a footballer*, is what she really meant. Which was true. Danny glanced, not over at Evie, but into the rear-view mirror, looked at himself looking at himself, turned his attention back to the road.

'I'm used to it now,' he said. 'It's like it'd be too much effort to start at this stage.'

'Have you ever taken a drink?'

'I'd a taste or two when I was younger. But the culture is serious over there. None of the lads touch alcohol or anything else, not the ones that make it, anyways.'

'I'm sorry, Danny. It's awful that a young fella not drinking is a rare enough thing it's worth remarking on.'

'You're the one doing the remarking.' Danny grinned.

'I suppose I am.'

'Don't worry about it.'

'I guess you can't miss what you never had.'

'That's it,' Danny said.

Evie looked like she was weighing up saying something else. Then she said it.

'Was it intense? Being over there?'

'It was intense enough. There was always a bit of an edge.'

'What was the edge?'

'You knew you were always a bad run of form away from trouble. That you were always under judgement.'

'The numbers are brutal, I'd say. The percentage of who makes it in the end.'

'They are.'

'Sorry. I must be wrecking your head.'

'Don't worry about it,' Danny said. 'Who are you meeting anyways?'

'Friends of mine, Amy Roche and Sandra Lavin. Do you know them?'

'I don't think so.'

'Before your time.'

Danny was driving slowly up Tone Street. As he approached Harrison's a taxi slipped out of the otherwise unbroken row of parked cars.

'Now that's some timing,' Evie said.

'We got lucky, all right.'

Danny drove a little past the vacated space, slung a pragmatic arm over the headrest of Evie's seat and swung the car into the gap.

'You're a gent, Danny,' Evie said, unclipping her belt. 'What time did you say Ben's train was in?'

'Six forty-five.' It was just gone six.

'Here, you've time yet. Come in for one if you want. A mineral or whatever.'

'Are you not meeting your friends?'

'That wouldn't preclude you coming in, but I'm not meeting them until eight. I just needed . . . a reprieve from my beloved family.'

'Eight,' Danny said. 'You're going to be stuck here for a while yet, so.'

'Oh, that doesn't bother me,' Evie said, opening the door and stepping out on to the pavement. 'Thanks again, Danny.'

## 3

Ben had got rid of the hair since Danny last saw him. His thick, dark mop of curls, gone. Shaven-headed, the planes of Ben's face looked starker, more ferocious, even when his expression was placid, as it was now, Ben checking his angles as he eased his chair off the exit ramp and on to the platform.

'All right,' Danny said.

'Well, dickhead,' Ben said, breaking into a grin.

'What's this?' Danny said, swiping his palm across Ben's crown, the stubble the pale brown of chocolate milk.

'Change your hair, change your life, brother.'

'Change it to what? You look like a convict.'

'And you look like your daddy,' Ben said, eyeing up Danny in his trousers and shirt.

'I'm a working man, now.'

'That you are.'

Ben paused and looked down along the tracks, travelling like a suture towards the horizon. Danny could already hear in his head every inflection of brotherly commiseration Ben might offer, from the incensed to the maudlin. What he wanted was for Ben to say nothing.

'It's good to see you,' was what Ben eventually said. 'I'm sorry I wasn't down sooner. They've been putting on extra shifts in *Eircom* all summer and I can't be saying no. This is my first weekend off in an age. You out from work long?'

'Finished at five, was just over at Shauna's.'

'How's Shauna?'

'She wasn't in.'

'How is she in general?'

'Good. The same,' Danny said, lifting Ben's laptop bag off his lap. A heavy-looking gym bag, full of dirty laundry presumably, was hanging from the rear of Ben's chair. Danny left the gym bag where it was. He went through the platform gate into the car park and Ben followed. They got to the car and Danny popped the boot, stashed the laptop bag over one wheel well. He opened the passenger door and stood in front of Ben. Ben leaned forward, Danny embraced him and had him in the car in a second. Danny unhitched the gym bag from the back of the chair, squished it in over the opposite wheel well, folded the chair and lifted it into the boot. Folding the chair took a couple of goes. It had been a while.

When Danny got in behind the wheel, Ben sniffed theatrically.

'Who's that perfume belong to? That's not Shauna's brand.'

'It's not, no.'

'Who?' Ben demanded.

'That's Evie Vaughan you're smelling.'

'Evie Vaughan!' Ben exclaimed.

'Like I said, I dropped over to the Vaughans'. Shauna wasn't there but Evie was. She needed a lift into town.'

'Who was she meeting in town? Was she meeting a fella?'

'She said friends.'

'Where'd you drop her?'

'Harrison's.'

'Harrison's! I would not say no to a drink in Harrison's.'

'That's where she went.'

'Evie Vaughan,' Ben sighed. 'It's strange. I was only thinking about her the other night, smoking out the window in the gaff in Drumcondra, listening to the foxes riding in the hedges. Evie Vaughan.'

'She has an appeal,' Danny admitted. 'She invited me in for a drink.'

Ben looked insinuatingly at Danny.

'She only wanted company. Said her friends weren't coming in until eight,' Danny said.

'And what did you say?'

'I said I'd to come here to get you.'

'Never mind me, man,' Ben said. 'God, that widowly melancholy off her. I can't say it's not sexy.'

'She's not technically a widow.'

'You ever hear foxes go at it? The yowling out of them. These blood-curdling, human-sounding screams. You'd swear someone was getting murdered in the bushes.'

'How's Dublin?'

'It's all right. I'm applying for every internship going.'

'You're planning to stay up there?'

'What am I going to do, come down here and run the website for the fucking dealership?'

Ben had finished his final year in college, graphic design in the Dun Laoghaire Institute of Art. He had originally wanted to do fine art. Painting stuff. The father wanted him to go into engineering. Graphic design was the compromise. Ben was now working in a call centre while he looked for a job that had anything to do with his degree.

'What was it made you cut your hair?' Danny asked.

'What's the big deal about me cutting my hair?'

'It's just. It seems extreme.'

'It occurred to me the hair on top of your head is the dead ends of it. Only the roots are alive, pushing the dead hair out. I was looking in the mirror one day and realised that for all these years I was carrying this big bushy corpse around on my head. So.'

Danny's phone started ringing.

'Sorry now, that's Shauna.'

'Go for it.'

'Hello,' Danny said into the phone.

'Where are you?' Shauna asked, sharp.

'I'm collecting Ben from the train station. Where are you?'

'I'm back home. Daddy said you were gone off with Evie.'

'Evie wanted a lift into Harrison's, so I gave her one.'

Ben punched Danny in the arm at that turn of phrase. Danny swatted at his brother to stop.

'That's awful chivalrous of you,' Shauna said. 'Are you there now?'

'I'm with Ben,' Danny said. 'He just landed in on the train. I've to drop him home.'

Ben squeezed Danny's arm and, when Danny looked at him, shook his head.

'Here, put her on speaker,' Ben said.

'I'm putting you on speaker,' Danny said into the phone. 'Ben wants to say something.'

'Hello Shauna,' Ben shouted.

'Hello, Ben,' Shauna said.

'Danny is absolutely not taking me home. We are going to go to Harrison's for a drink. Your sister said we could join her.'

'Did she, now?' Shauna said. 'Is that what you're doing, Danny?'

'That's what he's doing,' Ben said. 'The dickhead big bro down from Dublin is pulling rank. Come on in.'

Danny heard the crackle of a sigh from Shauna as she absorbed this information and another voice on the line.

'Who's there with you?' Danny asked her.

'Alice.'

'Hello Danny,' Alice shouted from Shauna's end.

'Welcome to the conference call,' Ben said. 'Will you tell that young one there that ye should come meet us in Harrison's?'

'I'll see what I can do,' Alice said. 'But you should know, we're heading out to Lacken in a bit.'

'What's happening in Lacken?' Ben said.

'You know the wind farm out there? They're putting a new blade on one of the turbines tonight.'

'OK,' Ben said, shooting Danny a bemused look.

'Da was with the escort that brought the blade out to Lacken today,' Alice continued. Her father was a Guard. 'He showed me a video off his phone. The thing is huge. It looks like a spaceship. They needed a special lorry to get it out there. It's getting attached tonight. I want to go see.'

'You're cracked, Lyons,' Danny said.

'I want to go too,' Shauna said.

'This is what you want to do with your Friday night?'

'It is.'

'Well, come meet us in Harrison's first,' Ben said.

# 4

Danny and Ben filed through the Friday-evening crowd. Busy enough, but Evie, with the reliable efficacy of a good-looking woman, had sourced and secured for herself a four-seater table near the back of the bar. Her face came out of the privacy of a thought as she looked up from her phone screen and registered the brothers' approach with a composed little start of attention. Danny instantly regretted having told Ben about Evie's offer, because he was sure now that it had been nothing more than a polite and therefore empty gesture. At least Ben was with him. He could blame Ben.

'Are you all right, Danny?' Evie asked him when they reached her table. She was smiling.

'What do you mean?'

'The puss on you.'

Danny glanced at the mirror behind the bar. He did not look upset. He did not look anything. His face looked only like his face; legible, in the sense that it said nothing.

'I'm fine,' he said.

'Ben, what did you do to your hair?' Evie asked.

'Joined a cult,' Ben said, blushing and grinning like a loon.

'Maybe a cult will put some manners on you.'

'How are you, Evie?'

'I'm out in public without a two-year-old welded to my hip for the first time in about six months, so I'm good. Did you track Shauna down yet?' she asked Danny.

'She got back to me, yeah. She's on the way here, actually, with Alice.'

'I will get you that drink.' Evie put up her hand at a passing server. 'Coke, or?'

'Diet.'

'Diet,' Evie said to the server. 'Ben?'

'I'll get a Guinness,' Ben said.

'You're still up in Dublin, Ben, doing . . . art?'

'Graphic design.' Ben shrugged. 'I'm finished college now and looking for gainful employment.'

'You have gainful employment,' Danny said.

'I mean a job that's actually in my field.'

'Good luck with it,' Evie said. 'I just started doing a bit of secretarial work, in at Ballina Town, in the office. It's only part-time, and it's only maternity cover, but I'm enjoying it.'

'You see Budgie McAllister in there much?' Danny asked.

'Budgie does be around,' Evie said with a smile. 'He's uh, one of a kind, that man.'

'He is all right,' Danny said. 'He hasn't asked you to put the squeeze on me yet, has he?'

Evie shook her head. 'He's after you, is he?'

'He'd like me to come play for them.'

'Well of course he would. Are you not going to?'

Ben chuckled.

'Danny's hardly going to go play for Ballina and have some hungover plumber from Belmullet break his ankle in a league match. He'll be back in England in no time.'

'No, I won't,' Danny said.

'What? Of course you're going to go back. You just need to get a couple of trials set up and you'll be flying—'

'I'm not going back. I'm here and I'm staying here.'

Danny tensed in his seat, took a long drink of his Diet Coke.

'What the hell are you going to do here?' Ben asked.

Danny showed Ben the palms of his hands.

'I'm doing it.'

'Doing what? Slinging Nissans for the oul fella?' Ben guffawed.

Danny smiled, rolled a mouthful of Diet Coke around in his mouth, the soft drink fizzling between his teeth.

'You got to start somewhere,' he said.


Presently, Shauna and Alice arrived. They were done up, strokes of eyeshadow coming out of their eye sockets like precise scorch-marks. Alice was a good-looking girl, but nobody looked like Shauna. Danny stood up off his seat and kissed her. As he drew back he tasted alcohol and limes on her breath, aseptic and greenly raw. Shauna drank, usually only in intense moderation, and though she never admitted it, Danny figured this habit of abstemiousness was out of consideration from him. Now she seemed – not drunk, but much closer to it than usual. He looked into her eyes and tried to divine how much she'd already put away, not that it bothered him; Shauna could do what she liked, and there was nothing wrong with her getting tipsy if she wanted.

'Good to see you,' he said.

'You too,' Shauna said.

'How was your day?'

'Grand now. Hung out with Al, mostly.'

'Well for some,' Danny said, though the remark sounded snider than he meant it to.

'Nothing to do at home. The B&B is dead today,' Shauna said defensively.

Shauna was ostensibly working for her parents for the summer, and even though, from what Danny could see, it was true that the place was rarely busy enough to warrant her presence, her parents seemed to be especially lax on her. Danny knew he shouldn't judge Shauna about her job, or how she applied herself to it, given he owed his own gig to bald-faced nepotism, though his oul fella did at least insist Danny worked every hour he was supposed to. But then Shauna's job was only a short-term thing, make-work before she headed off to college in September. The Leaving results weren't back for another few weeks but Danny knew Shauna was going to get the points. She had done well in her final exams, as she had all through secondary school, and was surely going to land her first choice, which was to study accountancy in Dublin City University.

Danny and Shauna had been boyfriend and girlfriend for four years. On the one hand, it did not seem as long as that, because Danny had been in Manchester around three-quarters of the time, and on the other hand, it seemed an age, because they had only been children, really, when they started going out. Their relationship had progressed as a series of staggered resumptions. They saw each other, were apart for a long time, then saw each other again. It was only this summer, when they could actually be together as much as they liked, that was the anomaly, and once Shauna headed to Dublin and Danny continued to stick it out in Mayo, their relationship would return to its remote and staggered pattern, but with their roles reversed. Danny stuck at home, Shauna away.

'Do you want to join us?' Evie asked Shauna and Alice.

'We do need to head if we want to get to Lacken in time,' Shauna said.

'The lads said something about the, uh, wind farm?' Evie asked.

'They're putting a new blade on one of the turbines. We're going to go check it out,' Alice said.

'You want to come?' Ben asked Evie.

Evie and Shauna exchanged glances.

'Enticing as the prospect of sitting in a field watching construction is, I think I'll leave ye to it,' Evie said. 'Despite what it looks like, I am actually meeting people here shortly.'

'How's all at home?' Shauna asked Evie.

'Dad is broken-hearted no one is there to eat the dinner with him.'

'Is Mam not back yet?'

'She wasn't when we left.'

'That woman better bring my car back in one piece.'

'Good thing you've this man,' Ben said, nodding at Danny. 'Ready to chauffeur anyone around at the drop of a hat.'

'Oh, I badgered him into that,' Evie said. 'I left him with no option.'

'Danny doesn't take much badgering,' Shauna said.

# 5

Lackan was several miles north of Ballina. Alice took Shauna in her car and Danny and Ben followed in Danny's car. The road to Lackan ran right along the coastline. For the majority of the drive you couldn't see the Atlantic, but you could feel it, the way the horizon just dropped clean off into the sky, gulls swirling like paper plates in the updraughts out over the low, invisible sea. Even though it was a Friday night, there was barely any traffic on the road. It was dusk by now, the sun a sinking ember in the sky, and in the rucked grades of the endless fields racing alongside the car the evening shadows lengthened and flickered like shutters at the edges of Danny's attention. Ahead of them the tail lights of Alice's car disappeared around a turn and presently reappeared each time the road straightened back up.

'Do you know how in gangster movies,' Ben said, 'there's always a scene where one car has to follow another car out somewhere secluded, into the woods or the desert or wherever?'

Danny glanced over at his brother.

'Everything all right with you two?' Ben asked.

'Me and Shauna?'

'Yeah.'

'Why?'

'Dunno. Just thought I was picking up a vibe in the pub there.'

'Shauna's been off with Alice for the day. They've had a couple of drinks. They're on their own buzz, you know.'

'Ah, don't mind me,' Ben sighed. 'It's not my place to say anything.'

'Well, thanks for not saying anything,' Danny said.

The wind farm was located on a flat, open stretch of land a quarter mile in from the sea. The access road into the farm was blocked off by a truck. Alice drove past the road and then turned down a lane beyond the wind farm, and Danny followed. A little further on the girls' car pulled in next to a small hill. Shauna and Alice were out and already cresting the hill by the time Danny had parked and helped Ben into his chair.

When they joined them at the top of the hill, the girls were taking hits off a hip flask and a joint. The smell of the joint was pungent.

'Shit. The ladies came prepared,' Ben said.

Alice offered Ben the joint and nodded out over the fields.

'It's going up.'

The wind farm was three fields away There were six

turbines. Each turbine had three blades, the blades of five of the turbines turning sedately in clean white strokes. The sixth was inactive. The damaged blade had been removed and the replacement, bound in a corset of cabling, was being lifted slowly through the air by a crane. Workers milled around at the foot of the turbine, their helmeted heads tilted up, watching the ascent of the enormous blade. The blade must have been a hundred-plus feet long. At the top of the turbine there was a large, socket-like cavity into which the blade was to be attached. They could see all this clearly in the dim of the dusk because the entire site around the turbine was lit up with spotlights. The scene was impressive, in one sense, but not the most compelling spectacle to take in over any length of time. It was, in the end, people doing work – slow work.

'What do you all think?' Danny asked.

'Shite,' Ben said, taking a bang off the hip flask.

'I think it's interesting,' Alice said, though even she didn't sound convinced.

Danny looked to Shauna. She was holding the joint. She took a drag and tipped her head back. Danny watched the muscles in her neck elongate and tauten as she held that position, then she brought her face back down level with Danny's and expelled a controlled current of smoke from her lips.

'I didn't know you were into that,' Danny said.

'I'm not,' Shauna said. 'You should take a hit.'

Danny's reflex was to say no. There was a zero-tolerance policy in the academy. You got caught with a trace of anything like that in your system and that was the end of you.

But so far as the academy was concerned, Danny was already ended. He frowned and took the joint, brought it to his lips and inhaled. The smoke was immediately unpleasant – too much of it, thick and cutting against the back of his throat – but he kept his lips shut and sucked it down into his lungs. The urge to cough welled in his chest, but he held his breath for a couple of seconds more before letting out a measured gasp.

'I'll be damned,' Ben said.

Danny handed the joint off to Alice.

Shauna was looking at Danny in a sullen way, like she had not expected, or even wanted, him to take the joint, even though she was the one who offered it.

'Let's go for a walk,' she said, and started off down the slope in the direction of the turbines before Danny could even answer. He followed and felt his heart begin to race. All around them, in the field they were walking through, the grass shimmered in huge silver chevrons where the coastal winds had rhythmically beaten it down.

'Are you all right?' Danny said when he caught up with her.

Shauna turned and glanced back at the hill, to make sure they were out of earshot of Alice and Ben.

'What is it?'

Shauna shook her head and pushed the heel of her palm into her eye. She was crying and trying not to cry. Shauna did not emote easily or often, and especially not in public.

'I didn't want to do this now,' she said, 'so I dared myself. I said, I know he won't take the joint. So I'll only say something if I offer him the joint and he takes it. And then you did.'

'What do you want to say?'

Shauna took her hands from her face, sniffed.

'I've been thinking about this for a while. How we've come to this point where, you know, I'll be heading to college and things are going to change for us, again.'

Danny was facing the inoperative turbine. He could see that the socket, the chamber, at the top of the turbine was roughly the size of a large room, because there were men in it, at least two. He could see the luminescent yellow rectangles of their high-vis vests moving back and forth on the edge of the socket, nothing but a clean drop beyond. They were surely in harnesses. The blade was rising towards them. It was going to dock, like a ship. Alice had called it a spaceship, hadn't she? And it did look like a ship or rocket, this tapered cylinder of sleek white material a hundred feet long, a rocket from the future. But why were the men up there? Just to observe, or were they going to help *guide* the thing into position? Even from this distance, Danny could see that the base of the blade, the section that was going to connect to the hub, was several times the diameter of a man. The blade itself must have weighed several tons. The idea that the affixing of this enormous object to the even more enormous object of the turbine came down to the intervention of a couple of human beings – the precariousness of that – was impossible for him to believe. Yet there they were.

Danny's scalp prickled as he imagined being one of them, all the way up there.

Shauna was still talking. She was talking about how they were going to be apart.

'We've always been apart,' Danny snapped. What he

meant was that so much of their relationship had already been long distance, that if they'd done it before, they could do it again.

'There's another thing,' Shauna said. 'It's hard to say. It's hard to put it in words. The way you've been, since you got back. And it's understandable, with how it ended over there for you.'

'And how've I been?'

'I don't know if it's fair for me to put a word on it, Danny. But you've not been yourself. You've not been the same, not to me.'

'How've I not been the same to you? I'm exactly the same.'

'You've been walking around like a zombie,' Shauna continued. Her voice had gone up a fraction, though she was still far from shouting, only speaking very clearly. 'It's like you're on autopilot, day after day. Every time I see you. Won't speak unless spoken to. Won't do anything unless I get you to do it. You nod and agree to things, to everything, but the look on your face. I have no idea where you are, but you're not here.'

'I'm here,' Danny mumbled.

His heart was still racing, in fact it was thumping now.

'I don't want it to sound like I'm ...' Shauna stopped, started again. 'I have my head to get straight. I have a life too. And I want to go into September knowing I don't have to be – worrying about you.'

Danny could see sparkles, flashes of silver and violet light. He closed his eyes and the sparkles transformed into sputters of yellow electricity. He was trying to control his breathing, in and out through his nose, because he felt like he might vomit. The curdling feeling in his stomach expanded in intensity. Seconds passed. It was only when he knew he wasn't going to be sick that he opened his eyes. Shauna's beautiful face was pale, welted and glossy with tears.

'Are you dumping me?'

Shauna scoffed. Wiped, with deliberation, at her cheeks.

'Danny, please don't be like that.'

'Like what?'

'Nothing's ended. Nothing's over. At least I don't want it to be. That's what's made it so hard to try and say anything, because of how you were going to take it.'

'Why are you crying if you're not dumping me?' Danny tried to smile but his lips just twitched.

'I'm crying because I'm sad.'

'You shouldn't be with someone who makes you sad.'

Shauna pressed her wrist into her nose.

'I'm going to go now, Danny. I'm going to head with Alice. Listen to me. I need some time, OK? Nothing's over, I just need some time. Do you hear what I'm saying?'

'Yeah,' he managed.

She kissed him, chastely, on the cheek, the wetness of her skin when she pulled away adhering like a decal to Danny's skin. She headed back towards the hill. Danny watched the turbine, the crane, the men hundreds of feet up in the air. When he knew Shauna would be far enough away he turned. He watched her pick her way up the summit, say something to Alice, then Ben, then Alice again, before the girls disappeared down the other side of the hill. Ben watched them go, then looked at Danny. Danny could feel the throb of his pulse in his temples. His head felt simultaneously heavy and airy. He realised he must be high. He didn't know what being high felt like, but maybe all it felt like was this. He waited until he heard the engine of Alice's car growl into life on the far side of the hill before he began to make his way back towards his brother.

## 6

'So you're saying she didn't dump you?' Ben asked.

The brothers were on the way back to Ballina. They had taken their time leaving Lacken in order to let the girls build an uncatchable lead, and Danny also wanted to make sure his head was clear enough to drive.

'She kept saying it's not over, but that she wants time to herself, time apart, something like that.'

'Goddamn. Did she say what was wrong?'

'She was talking about going off to college, needing her head straight for that—'

'Fuck off. So what? Everyone has to do that.'

'She said she thinks I've not been the same since I got home.'

'Not the same how?'

'In the way I'm acting, I guess.'

'Of course you've been different since you got home. People have experiences, they change,' Ben continued, gamely and loyally exasperated.

'She just needs some time to herself, was what she was getting at,' Danny said, but even as he said this, doubt was creeping in. With every second that passed it was becoming harder and harder for him to retain with any accuracy everything Shauna had said, much less put an order or logic on it. She had not dumped him, had denied it when he asked if that's what was happening. And yet Danny felt the exchange had the tenor of a dumping, of something breaking, irreparably. She'd walked away insisting she needed time. How could that mean anything good? If it was not a dumping, it seemed an awful lot like the prelude to a dumping.

'Them lads in the gangster movies,' Danny said after a while. 'That have to follow another car out to the desert. I assume nothing good comes of it?'

'You assume correct,' Ben said.

Just inside the town limits Danny stopped at a petrol station. He filled the tank at the pump then pulled into one of the parking spots. He was thirsty, could feel the dry clench of a headache coming on. He asked Ben if he wanted anything inside. Ben said no. There was an ice-cream freezer next to the soft drinks. Danny got himself a blueberry ice pop. He sat sideways in the driver seat of the car with the door open, his feet out on the forecourt concrete as he sucked away on the pop.

'You big baby,' Ben said over his shoulder.

'I am,' Danny said.

In the distance, above Nephin Mountain, the stars were appearing in the highest, darkest reaches of the sky. Danny wondered if he was still a little high, because the stars looked like mistakes, glimmering little misimpressions you assumed would not be there if you looked again, but they were. Danny was thinking about Shauna. It was Shauna's career adviser had first suggested accountancy.

She had talked it over with the parents and applied. No fuss, no messing about. That was Shauna all over. She was a reliable student, did not give her parents shit, treated her friends well, treated people in general well. If one of her friends fucked up, she made sure she was there for them. The flagrant, self-destructive gestures of adolescence held no attraction to her. She saw no point in working against her own best purposes. She possessed an innate level-headedness and faith that things were largely destined to turn out OK, and would do so as long as you did your part. The trick was to be able to figure out what your part was, and Shauna, in her quiet, sturdy, deliberate way, somehow seemed to know how to do just that. Danny had always admired that about her. He had always thought of her as someone who could see the world clearly, or at least reasonably, which meant that whatever conclusion she had come to about him was probably correct. *Zombie. Autopilot. Won't do anything unless I get you to. I have no idea where you are, but you're not here.*

A chunk of the ice pop slid off the stick and Danny held it in his mouth, letting it burn against the inside of his cheek before he swallowed it.

A car pulled in. He watched it glide across the fore-court, wondering why he had noticed it and realised too late who it belonged to as it stopped by a pump and the squat, enormous-arsed figure of Budgie McAllister emerged. Budgie saw Danny straight away. He slid his hands into the pockets of his dishevelled tracksuit, a track-suit that looked at least one size too big, and stared straight at Danny. He was wearing thick-framed glasses, his fea-tures scrunched up in what appeared to be an expression of anguish but which was due to the fact that the man was viciously short-sighted, or long-sighted, Danny could never remember.

He came over.

'There's Danny Faulkner, there's my number ten,' he said, no hint of a smile, no removing his hands from his pockets to offer Danny a handshake.

'Budgie. How are you?'

'You never answered my texts.'

'Sorry about that.'

'Training's Sunday. Come along. We've until the end of the month to register players for the new season.'

Danny grinned. The last of the ice pop was gone. He was sucking on the dye-stained stick.

'You don't stop, do you, Budgie.'

'Stop what?' he asked, with evident sincerity.

Budgie worked as a civil engineer, though it was hard to think of him existing in any capacity other than that of football coach. Danny remembers Budgie on the touchline of all those underage games; at times an engine of unending physical agitation, down on his haunches and bouncing on the soles of his feet, or pacing back and forth; at other times standing stock-still and staring at the action in a state of narcotic absorption, completely impassive but even then no more than the bounce of a ball away from his next eruption of scorn or bewilderment or furious joy. Budgie was charmless, obtuse, obstinate and unworldly. He lived inside the permanent childhood of football. Danny could not help but like the man.

Budgie just stood there, waiting.

'I've just, you know, I've been busy,' Danny said. 'I'm working full-time in the oul fella's dealership and—'

'All the lads have lives same as you, Danny. Playing for Town's not going to interfere with your job.'

'I know, but I'm still just getting into a routine and sorting out what I'll have time for . . .'

'You're a footballer. Come play football. Come be my ten.'

Danny dropped the pop stick on the ground between his legs and stamped on it, like it was a cigarette. He pushed his hands through his hair. 'Jesus, Budgie, if I say I'll come Sunday, will you leave me alone?'

'Of course not,' Budgie said. He did a little clockwise revolution, took in the entire forecourt and came back around to face Danny. Still no smile, his features still squinched up, but he looked, somehow, ecstatic. 'The lads are going to be just delighted you're back. We're going to absolutely fucking destroy Castlebar for the league this year.'

'I said Sunday, Budgie, I didn't promise anything else.'

'Sure thing,' Budgie said. He ducked down to look inside the car.

'Is that the brother?' he said to Ben.

'It is,' Ben said.

'Are you still giving them hell up in Dublin?'

'I am, Budgie.'

'Good stuff,' Budgie said, offering Ben a nod and withdrawing to his full height.

'Good to see you, Danny,' he said.

A car pulled up behind Budgie's at the pump and beeped. Danny watched Budgie, hand raised in apology, scuttle triumphantly across the forecourt.

## 7

The rest of the weekend was quiet – Danny went to the training session as he promised Budgie he would, though he was otherwise detectably down and kept to himself. A couple of times the folks asked him what had him in a mood and Danny deflected, though Ben reckoned they could fairly well guess, given how there was suddenly no sight nor mention of Shauna. Danny was processing and was best left to his own devices, was Ben's view. His little brother wasn't the most expressive lad but he was exquisitely sensitive. Things hit him and sunk down through him in stages and settled at the bottom of him for a long time. Ben tried to be a benign distraction, kept the talk small and innocuous whenever he sensed Danny was up for it. While he hoped Danny could work it out with Shauna, he also privately wondered if things had not run their natural course there. What Danny and Shauna had was young love, teenage love, first love, whatever you wanted to call it, and there came a time that kind of love had to end.

Speaking of love, Ben did do a local sweep of the apps on the off-chance Evie Vaughan was on there. It was awful sad what had happened to her, and she seemed sound, and she'd an arse on her Ben would eat like an apple if he got the chance. Not that he thought he'd have an actual chance; there'd be fellas lining up around the corner for Evie Vaughan if she was on the apps. In any case, he found no sign of her. Ben went back to Dublin that Sunday and did not get down to Ballina again until the end of September.

He bumped into Shauna on the Dublin train as it arrived at Manulla Junction. She was with a couple of young lads and young ones Ben didn't know and who didn't get off with her, they carried on to Castlebar. Shauna had faint green rings under her eyes and a queasy hesitancy around the mouth. Freshers' week, she explained. She'd been in Dublin a couple of weeks by then. Ben was a little cautious around her because he realised he wasn't sure if she and Danny were still together, or in what capacity. Once Ben had left Ballina back in July, he and Danny's communication had returned to its usual laconic pattern, amounting to little more than the occasional exchange of memes and videos, Ben a couple of times asking, but only as a formality, how Danny was and Danny shooting back a perfunctory 'grand' or a thumbs-up emoji.

There was a match on that Saturday, Ballina at home against Foxford. Ben went in with JJ to watch. There was a crowd of maybe eighty people, and Shauna and Alice were there too. Alice was in college in Galway.

The weather could be beautiful in September in the west, but that afternoon was sombrely autumnal; above the pitch a sheet-metal sky out of which descended a drizzle so fine it seemed less to fall than to hang in the air in an atomised mist, powdering your face with dampness.

Ballina were in their home kit of all white with black trim, Danny wearing '10' on his back, the oddball Mc-Allister watching from the touchline. It wasn't a great game, though what could you expect? Danny, the only lad without a hint of a beer gut, was the best technician out there by a mile. Again and again he came into possession of the ball, feinted smooth as silk into space and threaded passes right on to the toes of his teammates, whereupon the ball was either miscontrolled, punted straight back to the opposition or blazed into touch.

As the game went on, Ben kept stealing glances up at Shauna, watching her alternate between paying attention to the game and conferring with Alice. He studied her face for clues about what she was thinking, but the thing about a face was that you could read anything you wanted into it. What Ben wanted was to take Shauna aside and tell her to do whatever she liked with her life but not to fuck about with his little brother in the meantime.

The game was 1–1 with ten minutes left when Danny decided it. Ballina won the ball in the middle of the park. Danny, on the edge of the Foxford penalty box, with a great lunk of a centre half climbing all over his back, let the ball roll to him and flicked it first time with the toe of his boot up over his right shoulder. The centre half could only watch the ball float over his head, close enough that for a moment he could have reached out and touched it, as Danny spun instantly left and was there to collect the ball before it touched the turf on the other side of the stricken centre half. As he did so, the covering centre half lunged at him. Danny took a calm, almost decorous, step out of his path and in the same movement rifled the ball cleanly across the keeper and into the net. A cheer erupted from the crowd and Budgie punched the air.

'That's it, Danny!' JJ shouted.

'Nice goal,' Ben said, 'but he should be scoring three a game against this shite.'

'I know,' JJ said.

Danny, who did not react at all at first, evaded the

attempted embraces of a couple of teammates and made a
run for the touchline. He came up past Budgie and the two
casually high-fived, then he kept going until he reached
Shauna. Ben saw the smile on Danny's face – knowing,
embarrassed and determined – as he pulled her close and
kissed her and a second, demented bellow of cheers
and ironic jeers came up from the crowd. A teammate
jumped on Danny's back and a couple of nearby teenage
boys leaped in. Danny let Shauna go and stepped back so
she wouldn't get clobbered. For a moment Danny reared
up under the weight of this mob of celebrants, and then he
gave in, falling to his knees as more bodies piled on.

Ben did not see Danny much for the rest of that weekend.
Danny spent most of his time at Shauna's, though he did
promise to drop Ben to the train station on the Sunday
evening. By the time Danny and Ben hit the road they
were running a little late because lunch at the Vaughans
had run over. The route into town, as it always did, took
them past the spot where JJ and Ben had had their accident all those years ago. The spot was completely
unremarkable, an anonymous stretch of road with a verge,
a ditch, nothing but listing telegraph poles and fields of
grazing sheep in the distance. Ben had been four. He could
not remember anything about the crash. What
he does know is that JJ had been working on the produc-
tion line of the bakery factory over in Foxford at the time
and he still found it funny, and completely in keeping with
their father's character, that despite being seriously and
permanently maimed in a car crash in which his firstborn
son was even more grievously injured, JJ subsequently

took up selling cars for a living, and did it with sufficient success to end up buying a majority stake in a dealership. But that was how their father was, pragmatic to the point of annihilation. Things and feelings that were no longer of use he dispensed with, and that's what the past was. A thing that was no longer of use.

Ben was like his father in that regard. He remembers Danny asking him about his shaven head back in the summer, wanting to know why he had chopped all his curls off. Ben hadn't told anyone in his family, but it was over a woman. The woman had left him. She had loved his hair and so, once she was gone, he had decided the hair had to go too. Nobody in the family had known about her while Ben was seeing her. He had liked keeping the relationship for himself. While Ben still viscerally equated Ballina with home, the place he could always come back to if, as had happened to his little brother, everything fell apart, his actual life was now in Dublin. Even after the woman had left him, that life had not fallen apart. He had not let it.

They entered the town limits. Lawns and their houses, commercial properties, estate greens, turn-offs, car parks and petrol stations slid by Ben's window in the same configuration they always did. Danny was going on about his plans for later. He was taking Shauna to the cinema, which meant Shauna was not heading back to Dublin until the morning.

'Looks like it's rosy enough with you and Shauna, anyway,' Ben said.

Danny gave Ben a dubious look.

'No?'

Danny shrugged.

'We're giving it a go,' he said. 'When she's down here I'm with her and when she's up there, it's – whatever. The rule is we don't make a deal of it. That's how we're doing it for now.'

Ben wasn't sure how to take that – the big-brother's interrogative instinct flared up in him for a second – but he let it go. He glanced at the dashboard clock.

'We're cutting it fine for this train, actually.'

'Don't worry about it,' Danny said, hitting the accelerator.

'How's the season going with Town? Are ye going to win the league?'

'If we don't, we'll get mighty close.'

'Ye'll do it so.'

'When we do it,' Danny said, 'then it'll be done.'

'You seem good, though.'

'I'm all right. But how are you? Are you doing OK?'

'You know me, I'm a moody pup at the best of times.'

'You're a man in a hurry,' Danny said. 'You want things.'

'Doesn't everyone?' Ben said, but Danny didn't answer, just watched the road.

Soon they were at the station. Danny drew up level with the entrance, flicked on the indicator and waited for a break in the traffic coming the other way. When the break appeared, he swung them into the station's car park. As soon as they entered it they could see that the train was still there, the same two little carriages as ever with their sets of doors open, the people gathered on the platform – people Ben, without even having to look, knew he knew – stepping on board with no particular urgency.

'What did I tell you,' Danny said. 'We made it.'

# ACKNOWLEDGEMENTS

I would like to thank the Irish Arts Council, The Toronto Arts Council and Jill Morrison and everyone at the Rolex Mentor Protégé Arts program for their assistance and support during the writing of this book.

Everyone at Cape and Grove Atlantic, in particular Nick Skidmore and Katie Raissian, and Jordan Ginsberg at Strange Light.

Several of the stories in *Homesickness* first found a home in various magazines. I would like to thank Cressida Leyshon, Deborah Treisman and Adrian Kneubuhl for their careful and rigorous eyes.

Thank you to Lucy Luck and Anna Stein, who go above and beyond.

Thanks to Paul, Tim, Oisin, John Patrick, Tom, Lisa, Nicole, Declan, Sean, Gavin and Colm, among many others, for knowing when to talk and not talk about the work, and for being legends in general.

And finally, thank you to my family, for always being there, and for putting everything in perspective.